Wolf's Christmas

Papa-T Productions

Wolf's Christmas

A Christmas Story of renewed Faith, Hope, and Love.

TODD DAYTON FOX

Wolf's Christmas

A Christmas Story of renewed Faith, Hope, and Love.

ISBN Paperback: 978-0-9980757-5-4

ISBN EBook: 978-0-9980757-8-5

Copyright © 2020 by: Todd Dayton Fox (Papa-T)

Published by Todd Dayton Fox and Papa-T Productions
www.papa-t-pro.com

Rev2021

EXPRESSIONS OF GRATITUDE
Wolf's Christmas

Patrick Schartz
Whose character was the inspiration behind this wonderful
story. Patrick Schartz was a wonderful father, a kind friend,
and an iconic Santa, influencing a Christmas Fantasy
Adventure unlike any other story ever told.

Karen Fox
Austin Fox, Diana Seitz, and George Seitz
Monty and Lesa Fox
Michelle and Wayne Gwin
Melissa and Raymond Long

The Schartz family
Kathy, Jennifer, and Patrick Jr.

Santa Claus, and to all the Santa's across the Big-Wide-World!

Table of Contents

CHAPTER ONE..7

CHAPTER TWO..25

CHAPTER THREE..37

CHAPTER FOUR..61

CHAPTER FIVE..71

CHAPTER SIX..95

CHAPTER SEVEN...117

CHAPTER EIGHT..143

CHAPTER NINE..161

CHAPTER TEN..175

CHAPTER ELEVEN..195

CHAPTER TWELVE...209

CHAPTER THIRTEEN..227

CHAPTER FOURTEEN...247

CHAPTER FIFTEEN...255

CHAPTER ONE

CHRISTMAS EVENING

Just as the local meteorologists had predicted, the blizzard that was forecast a week prior began to emerge on the horizon, right as Christmas evening was drawing closer to its end. The last glimpse of the galaxies hovering above the earth vanished over the mountainous terrain, while the dark clouds from the approaching storm began towering through the skies. Exploding into the heavens, the storm had diminished any chance the villagers had for a calm and peaceful night. It did not take long for the stillness of the evening to grow dark and cold, just as if God himself had blown out the stars like delicate candles. The wind grew strong; blowing everything in its path. Between the black sky and the heavy snow, it was nearly impossible for any unfortunate soul, who might still be out in the elements, to see what was directly in front of them.

For the most part, all of the town's residents remained at home to enjoy the company of their families for the holiday. It was the wish of their master that everyone remain in their homes on Christmas, nonetheless, some of the men had an important job to do that required a few hours of their time. For those individuals, their presence was required until the special task they had been summoned for was complete. The newly arrived blizzard was so dense that there was no longer any visibility to speak of. Some of the men that attended the ranch had been gathered outside for some time. They had assembled at the town's stables, waiting in the arctic winds, trying desperately to stay warm. The ranch hands were anxiously expecting the arrival of their employer and his hitch team, who had set out the day before. The men were well aware of their master's itinerary and knew his arrival was well overdue. He had been scheduled to return, well before this evening's snow began to fall.

For every minute that the men waited, it seemed as if a lifetime had passed in the bitter cold. The men huddled together for only a hint of warmth, but as they attempted to remain patient, a sense of worry began to grow heavy on their hearts. Although the men were eager to get out of the frigid weather, the ranch master's loyal crew refused to leave their positions. They had dismissed any loss of hope for his safe return. The men loved their employer and wanted nothing more than to see him arrive back at the ranch safely.

Anxious for his boss's welfare, the ranch manager, John Dreiling, could not handle sitting in place any longer. He stood himself upright in the wind and walked over to pick up the rotary phone, hanging on the wall next to where he had been waiting. Upset about the current situation, he could not understand why Dispatch had not updated him for over an hour. Dreiling called the office to see if there was any word from their master. Shaking his head, Mr. Dreiling did not get the answer he had been hoping to receive. He hung up the phone and returned his focus into the evening sky. With all his might, he watched and listened for any signs of life that he could possibly see or hear. As he made his move, everyone turned their heads and kept their eyes directly on him. They knew that Dreiling would be the first to see their master so they needed to remain vigil at all times. For once he did, he would be signaling the boys to begin hustling into place for the big retrieval.

Knowing that the scheduled time of his master's arrival had come and gone. After what seemed like eternity, Mr. Dreiling reached into his coat with his aching cold hand and pulled out his pocket watch to view it. He broke from his attention only long enough so that he could look down at the time, letting out a heavy sigh as he just stared in to the face of the watch. Concerned, and unsure what to do, he looked back up and turned to the men at the stable gates. They could read his body language well, as they all feared the same thoughts as their manager. They knew it was time to declare an emergency for their master. Reluctantly, Mr. Dreiling began to raise his hand to give the signal to his crew, but just as he began to make his move, there was a turn of events, and a familiar sound of bells began to ring out through the strong winds.

Without a moment of hesitation, the men quickly came to attention as the glow from the dim light began to appear from out of the darkness, growing in intensity until the light pierced brightly, emerging out of the blowing snow. Their precious cargo had arrived. Relief quickly overpowered the men's anxieties as a rush of adrenaline gave the crew their second wind. Although fatigue had moved in on everyone involved, smiles instantaneously appeared on their faces as they looked to their manager for guidance. John Dreiling began waving his arms to the others, and everyone made their way to their assigned positions, assuring the safe arrival for their chief and his rig.

Not far from the stables, the master's wife sat in her bedroom awaiting the return of her husband. Although she knew this was an important tradition for everyone in the entire city, she still could not control the feeling of helplessness and fear that had overcome her. No different from any of the years past, she tried her best to keep her mind off her spouse's dangerous journey, desperately managing to find comfort as she waited. She held a cup of cocoa in her hands and read from her book, lit dimly from her lantern that was beginning to run low on fuel. Christmas day for the master's wife was not spent in the same fashion as most of the world. For her, Christmas was spent in isolation, without friends or family. There were no Christmas morning celebrations for her to wake up to, and there was no Christmas ham on the table to share with the family. For her, the entire holiday was spent away from her husband in wait for his return. For most, a partnership with this type of arrangement would simply end in catastrophe. For this marriage, however, there was a greater importance to be considered, and for that, she remained loyal to her husband and respected his calling.

Just as soon as she heard the faint voice of Mr. Dreiling outside, calling out commands to the rest of the men, she rose from her chair and darted to her window. With a rush of relief, she grabbed the curtains and drew them aside quite harshly, almost ripping them from their rods. She then peeked outward, just in time to watch her spouses sleigh pull into the ranch and come to a stop at the stables. With a sigh of relief, she looked up into the heavens, beyond the winter storm, and gave a quick prayer of Thanksgiving, acknowledging the Lord above for once again, bringing her husband home safely to her. Not wanting to make her husband feel bad for his late arrival, she stepped away from the window so that he would not see her looking outward. She knew that if he spied her looking on, he would recognize the fear in her eyes and would feel guilty for keeping her waiting on him under these conditions. Out of his sight, she sat on the bed where a rush of emotions came over her. She was elated that he was safe but at the same time, she was upset with him for continuously risking his life in those deadly cold winds. With an overwhelming sense of happiness, she began to cry in anger.

Although the passing years had made her a strong woman, she could not help but to allow herself a few moments to discharge her emotions and let the tears fall across her cheeks. However, once she was done, she regained her composure and reached for her lantern to blow out the flickering light. Her husband was safe, and that was all that mattered to her. She would see her bridegroom soon enough, but would not be waiting up any longer. Finally satisfied that her spouse was in good hands, she crawled underneath her blankets and fell to sleep in her weariness.

As the master and his team rode into the farmyard, arriving at the stables, the men spared no time rushing to receive them. They needed to act quickly to get the rig out of the bitter cold. The sleigh was covered with ice, which disabled the devices on board that the crew relied on to produce heat for the pilot and his animal team. As the men approached the sleigh, a tall and mighty looking man stood up from within the rig. High above the rest, he looked around to see the operations unfolding around him and then he climbed down from his hitch. The master's men greeted him as they retrieved the frozen vehicle. In return, he thanked them for their help and passed the hitch over to the crew to care for.

The crew immediately went to work on their post ride inspections, as their employer walked around to each of the reindeer to check on their health. The master was known for his ability to speak and communicate with animals. He did not want to leave them until he knew they were safe, so one at a time, he placed his cold hands on their shoulders and spoke silently to them. The old man loved his team of caribou very much. He thanked each of his stag personally for their sacrifices, because without them, the man would not have been able to accomplish his mission.

After assuring his sleigh and his team were in good hands, the master found his manager. He shook his hand and thanked him for caring for the ranch during his absence. He then turned from the stables and retreated to his nearby office so that he could permanently get out of the cold. The man had been out in the elements for over twenty-four hours. The journey had been long and rough. He was happy that his mission was finally complete; however, he still had one last item to check off of his list before he could even think about retiring for the day. While the details of the trip were fresh in his thoughts, he wanted to start his report and cover the highlights of his expedition. The trip had been a successful one, yet, it did not go without its fair share of undesired surprises. There were many concerns about his journey that he wanted to make note of, in hopes of better outcomes for future missions.

Once the man was inside his office, he pulled off his hat and gloves, placing them on his desk, and then removed his coat to hang it on the rack along the wall. He looked as though he had just been through a war, with his uniform covered in soot, and exposing several damaged areas on his coat where he had fringed the fabric by getting too close to fiery elements.

The calm steady flame from his fireplace had been the only thing that kept his office warm while he was away. He shut the door to his room, allowing the heat to rush over him, welcoming the cold soul back home to the ranch.

Sitting down at the desk, he went through his pockets to make sure he didn't lose anything along the way. He remembered that he had found something during his journey and pulled it out of his pouch. He held in his shaky hands, an old ring that he had discovered. Fumbling to get a good look at it, the man sat in thought as he gazed upon it. He then placed it on his desk next to the lantern, very gently, as if it had some importance to him.

The tired man then grabbed his lantern and lit it so he could use it to write by. While he sat at his desk, the man attempted to find something to write with so that he could work on his trip log. He looked through all of his drawers for a working pen, but as he searched unsuccessfully for it, he began to grow angry and his frustration began to get away from him. The man was tired and physically exhausted.

Looking around to make sure he was alone; an unexpected welling of emotions came over him. He began to breathe rapidly and heavily from a sudden burst of anxiety. Trying to calm down, he began to cough out the frigid air from his cold lungs and attempted to replace it by taking deep breaths from the warmer air inside. The man's exhaustion soon brought him to a state where he was no longer able to contain himself. He began to cry at his desk, as the events of the last day had taken a demanding toll on the man's body. Although he was not known as someone who showed those types of emotions, his physical and mental self were simply too weak to fight off the tears.

He had no desire to be found during a moment of weakness, so after a couple of long deep breaths, he managed to settle himself before someone discovered him. Once calmed, he looked down, only to find the pen he had been searching for. The pen was sitting there in plain sight, in the middle of his desk, where it had probably been the entire time. He pulled out his logbook and began writing, trying to take his mind off of his aching body. Even though he stumbled to hold the pen with his cold fingers, he continued to try his best. As he wrote on, Mr. Dreiling entered the dimly lit office and sat in the chair across the room, remaining quiet, as not to interrupt his master. The man's assistant sat patiently for quite some time, making no attempt to disturb his boss as he continued writing in his log. As he sat he watched his master, looking for signs of health issues from his journey. The man was a quiet person, but he was also very observant.

After some time, the master let out an exhausted sigh, and looked up and over to Mr. Dreiling. "Well, overall, the trip went well. There were a few issues worth mentioning but we accomplished our goal. Also, the animals did an outstanding job as usual... God bless their hearts."

Placing his hands over his tired face, the old man sighed again, steam continuing to rush out of his mouth from his still cold lungs. He reached into his pocket and pulled out a felt pouch. From within the bag, he gently pulled out a hand carved pipe and held it in front of him. With his frigid hands he tried to fill the pipe with tobacco so that he could smoke from it. At first, his shaky fingers refused to cooperate with his desire to light the craft, but the man refused to give up, trying to remain calm. Finally, after a few more moments in the warm air, he began to grow steady and he successfully lit the antique vessel. He then put the pipe in his mouth and took a deep draw.

Looking over to Mr. Dreiling he decided to give him a short synopsis of the trip, just for the evening. "I don't think I have many more years in me to do this trip safely on my own. Each year the cold air seems to get increasingly unbearable and the people seem to be growing angrier, almost violent. We need to start thinking about getting some help, and soon. I never thought I would ever utter these words, but I am getting too old to continue with this much longer."

With that, his assistant was content enough; just to know that there were no immediate medical issues that his boss needed attended to. He nodded his head, stood up from his chair, and smiled at his employer as if to say "it's good to have you home." Reaching into his pocket, he pulled out a small package and sat it on the desk in front of his employer. As he leaned forward, he glanced at his boss's log and saw that the writing was barely legible from his cold fingers. He then turned and left the room just as quietly as he had entered.

The gentleman chuckled and reached over to pick up the package that was wrapped in wrinkled gifting paper, obviously scarred from the long wait in the cold air. His fingers were still slightly shaky, hindering his ability to remove the ribbon and paper from the package. Holding the box up higher, he tilted it and looked inside to see what was within the wrapping. Closing his eyes a couple times to clear his blurred vision, he reached over and put on a pair of glasses so that he could get a better look. Lying silently was a small wooden train car. Each year the ranch employees gifted him a new car, adding it to a train set they had made for him years ago. Proudly, he placed it at the end of his train, making it forty cars long.

Too weak to even make his way up the hill to the house so that he could find his bride, the old man made his way to the window and peeked out and looked through the trees, trying to see if there were any lights on in the house. He knew that if there was any light at all, that his wife would be awake and he did not want her to be concerned for him. He smiled, knowing she was resting. Walking back to his desk, he sat down and placed his hands behind his head, as he leaned back into his chair. While he watched the flames dance on the walls around him and listened to the popping sounds echo about from the burning logs, his eyes began to grow uncontrollably heavy. In just a fraction of a moment's time, the man fell asleep at his desk in exhaustion. And, just like that, Christmas had concluded.

THE FOLLOWING SEPTEMBER

September was an overly welcomed month for the agricultural community of Ellinwood. With the ever-growing heat of summer, not one single person could stand the hot climate any longer. Everyone was eager for cooler temperatures as they prayed hard for signs of autumn to begin. For the third year in a row, the farmers were experiencing several failed harvests. Little rainfall and extreme heat brought no hope for the agriculturalists as they helplessly watched their crops wither and die in the scorching hot winds. Along with the drought stricken farmland, followed an overall drop in the economy. With every crop lost, more and more families began losing sizable savings. Other families had lost their incomes all together and were struggling, day after day, to make ends meet. Although this was a time of tribulation for the community, everyone had one commonality in that they were excited for the summer season to come to an end.

Ellinwood was no different from that of any other small mid-west farming town. The people were friendly and everyone did what they could to take care of one-another. Far from the complexities of the big city, Ellinwood lay deep within the ocean of prairie land and the endless waves of fields. The farmers of Ellinwood were responsible for raising several crops during the summer and autumn months. The grain they produced would eventually be shipped throughout the lands, feeding the people of the world. The Ellinwood residents were very caring and kind to one-another, but when it came to friendly people, Patrick Wolf was the kindest of them all.

Patrick Wolf, a local business man, looked up from his office desk to spy his clock. It was nearly closing time, and after a long day, Patrick was ready to head home and enjoy the evening with his wife. One sure sign that fall was around the corner was the beginning of the local high-school football practices. Knowledge that the kids were beginning to meet each afternoon to prepare for the upcoming season brought a sense of reassurance to the locals. For them, it meant that cooler temperatures were right around the corner. To Ellinwood and the surrounding districts, football was more than an exciting game to end a brutal work week. Football season also meant that the preparation for the next year's crops was also soon to start, and new beginnings meant new hopes for a recovering economy. Each evening Patrick would make his daily commute home, passing by the stadium hoping to catch a glimpse of the athletes practicing on the field.

For Patrick, not only was the beginning of after-school practices a sure sign of the end of summer, but it was also his queue to prepare for the upcoming Christmas season. Wolf loved Christmas, and he loved the months leading up to his favorite day. His passions for the fall and autumn months were extremely contagious to everyone that knew him, creating a wide-spread feeling of joy around the entire community. Patrick was a local unknown hero. He was Ellinwood's local Santa Claus figure, and he cherished the coveted position very highly. Every one of the town's young adults grew up with Mr. Wolf as their Santa, and over the years he established a unique bond with everyone in the community.

The holiday seasons of fall and winter brought back many cherished memories of Patrick's childhood, as well as many wonderful remembrances of Christmas. Patrick loved being the town Santa with all his heart. However, over the past few years, Patrick couldn't help but feel that the joy within the children seemed to be fading away. The wonderful feelings he experienced with each of the passing holidays, leading up to Christmas morning, he no longer felt were shared with the local community. Patrick felt the spirit of Christmas was being forgotten. Chaos and anger, around the world, seemed to replace Christmas joy through the stresses of everyday life.

He always held the Holidays as a time for families to be together. But each year, as everyone grew older, his time with his children diminished, as they were spending more time with their own families.

Patrick felt that everyone he knew was beginning to dismiss the beloved holiday spirit and the Christmas culture he had struggled to pass on. It seemed to him that those beliefs were now considered old fashion and no longer relevant to the younger generations. They were no longer continuing many of those traditions with their own children. Patrick began to lose hope in the future of Christmas and he struggled with it a great deal. You see... Christmas was so much a part of Patrick that when he began to see the spirit dyeing through others, he felt a sense of failure in his purpose to spread the joys of the holiday to the community.

As the sun sat on the horizon, Patrick and his wife Katie were enjoying a quiet evening together. Katie had prepared a large meal for she and Patrick, as she routinely did each evening. The two would discuss the day, updating one-another about everyone they knew. They shared the laughs, as well as the tears, through each and every story that was reminisced between them. Patrick and Katie were childhood sweethearts. They raised a beautiful family, creating wonderful memories along the way. Now their children were raising families of their own and Patrick and Katie were delighted to be the grandparents to such wonderful kids.

After dinner, the two would retire to the living room to watch a little television for the remainder of the night.

This evening, Patrick's heart was unsettled. He made an attempt to shake it off by taking a short nap. However, as he awoke, he still felt the sense of anxiety overwhelming him. He leaned over, kissed Katie on her forehead, and excused himself from the living room. He then walked to the bedroom and approached the closet. Opening its doors, he reached in and pulled out an old trunk from the darkness. With great care, he sat the trunk on the luggage rack at the foot of the bed and opened it slowly. He then took a step back and just stared into it. He slowly grinned as he looked inside. After a few moments had passed, Katie became curious as to what Patrick was up to. She poked her head into the room and noticed Patrick standing in front of the bed, gazing at the contents within the trunk.

Smiling, she leaned against the threshold of the door and watched as he looked on. "Your suit is just as beautiful today as it was the first day we brought it home."

Startling Patrick and breaking his train of thought, Patrick's grin slowly drifted away into some far off place. "Does anyone even know what this is anymore? I don't know honey... Maybe it's time to pack this away for good."

Katie knew her husband was contemplating giving up one of his most cherished items. She felt heartbroken and wanted nothing more than for Patrick to find the old Christmas spirit that made him so young inside. Katie put her hand on Patrick's shoulder as the two remained quiet and stared into the trunk. Many wonderful memories filled their heads as they looked at the precious items inside.

Looking inside Patrick's trunk was like gazing at a hypnotic sea of crimson and shimmering metals. Lying on top was a black leather belt with a shiny buckle, plated in twenty-four-carat gold. The buckle was so big that the reflection from the light above seemed to make the room brighter. The belt lay on top of a brilliant red suit, trimmed with various shades of red embroideries and white fur. Along with the suit was a pair of black leather boots, also with gold buckles fastened around the ankles.

Inside the trunk was Patrick's Santa suit. The uniform had been well used and many places of the suit had worn spots. But with each tear and behind every blemish, there was a special story to be told. Opening the Santa trunk was always a moment of excitement for Patrick. For every year, at the first glance inside the trunk, a lifetime of smiling faces would rush back to Patrick and overwhelm him with happiness, validating his passion to be the town Santa.

However, this year seemed much different. This year the smiling faces still greeted him, but this time, there were no new memories remembered from just one year ago, and it bothered Patrick very much. In fact, it brought upon a sense of sadness. It upset him so much he began to wonder why he was getting the suit out at all this year.

Patrick looked down to the floor, away from the items inside the case. With a sigh, he opened up to Katie. "I bet if I never wore this again, no-one would even care."

Closing the lid and gently wiping the layer of dust from the top of the case, Patrick pushed the trunk back into the closet and slowly closed the door. Katie placed her gentle hand on her best friend's shoulder and as they shut the light off to their room, the two returned to the living area and spent a quiet evening together, cuddled tightly in each other's arms. And as they enjoyed the night, Katie said a silent prayer for her husband, asking God to help Patrick find his renewed excitement as Santa again.

CHAPTER TWO

THANKSGIVING

The Wolf household felt like home again as the entire family gathered in Ellinwood for a weekend of thanksgiving and fellowship. Patrick and Katie's children, Jena and Patrick Junior, had returned home the day before Thanksgiving for one of the family's most time-honored weekends. It had become tradition for the family to reunite and attend the yearly high school musical production together. They would then share Thanksgiving together as one happy family. With the smell of turkey in the air and grandchildren running throughout the house, it was impossible to not feel an overflowing sense of joy in their hearts.

The time for dinner had arrived. Katie had prepared a perfect holiday feast for her treasured gifts. As soon as the last of the fixings were completed, she called out the dinner invitation to her family. Everyone in the household rose from their seats and rushed to the dining room, anxiously gathering around the table. This year, Patrick Junior said grace. Everyone bowed their heads as he spoke about all the blessings they had shared together over the past year. Katie's heart was full, knowing that her children had grown into such wonderful parents and were passing on their love of God to their offspring. After the blessing was concluded, Katie reached over and turned on some dinner music for everyone to enjoy. And with that, conversation and laughter filled the entire house, as everyone began to feast upon the Thanksgiving turkey.

The dinner was a success. Everyone filled their plate to full capacity and fed upon the holiday meal. However, as the moments passed, Patrick subconsciously grew quieter. His mind had been racing about other things that were concerning him. And soon, he slowly began to withdraw from the conversation all together. Jena could not help but notice that her father was not his usual self. She had witnessed the mood of her hero wither away within a matter of moments. Knowing that this was not her dad's usual self, she could not help but to seek understanding.

Jena cautiously interrupted the dinner table conversation. "Daddy, are you ready for the big month? The kids keep telling me how excited they are for Christmas. They can't stop talking about what they plan to tell Santa when they see him this year."

Patrick responded with a nod but did not answer her. Jena looked over to her mother, who was looking back at her with a meek smile, which seemed rehearsed at best.

Her daddy's quiet reaction had finally upset Jena and she nearly dropped her utensils with frustration. She just couldn't take seeing her father so unusually quiet any longer. "Daddy, what's wrong? Is everything alright?"

Reluctantly, Patrick told his family that he was thinking of retiring his Santa suit this year. He looked over at his grandchildren, who were laughing and having a good time at the other table. Under his voice he told his wife and children not to worry about it, and that he was sure there were plenty of helpers out there who will make sure the kids get to see Saint Nick this year.

Jena had never known her father to pass up playing Santa for the children. She and Patrick Junior were a bit dismayed by his news. Patrick's Santa role was responsible for some of their greatest memories together, so they were not happy with what they had just heard.

Feeling sad for Patrick, she stood up and walked around to her father. "I love you daddy. It's just not going to be the same without our beloved Santa."

Although Thanksgiving dinner was wrapping up and everyone was shocked about what their father had just told them, the subject was changed and the day continued. The men watched the annual professional football game on the television and Jena went outside to take a walk with her mother. Concerned for her daddy, she asked again if everything was okay with him. Katie told her what Patrick had said to her about his uncertainties, continuing as Santa. He had just turned a half a century old this year, so Katie felt that he was simply undergoing some sort of midlife crises. She held the belief that after a year off, he would begin to miss his role and next year would return to his suit and be a better Santa than ever before. Jena could grasp her dad's feelings and agreed with her mother. She decided not to dwell over it any longer and prayed that her father would find his way back to his old self.

The family did not return to the Santa conversation for the remainder of the weekend. They simply enjoyed each other's company and made new memories together as a family, however, concerns of Patrick's decision was never far from their minds.

THE ANNUAL CHRISTMAS PARTY

The following Monday, Patrick and Katie were attending the city Christmas party at the lodge. The night of the party was also the evening when the city tree was to be lit, setting off the Christmas season for the small community. For the first year, Patrick was going to attend the party without playing Santa Claus for the children. Although he was indeed a little saddened by stepping down as the jolly soul, he had never had the opportunity to spend the entire evening in celebration with Katie, so he was heartened with the thought of being able to enjoy the evening and savor the time with his wife.

Katie suggested to Patrick that they park closer to the downtown square, where they were planning to light up the tree. This way they could avoid the parking lot that was closer to the event center. The Ellinwood Christmas parties had a reputation for their merry celebrations, so Katie thought it would be the safer bet to park away from the crowd. Once they found the perfect spot, they came to a stop where they spied a few of the city crew men finishing up preparations for the lighting ceremony. Patrick got out of the vehicle and walked around to the passenger side to help Katie out of the van and onto the sidewalk, just a single block from the lodge.

The two looked their best as they dressed up for their first ever Christmas party as a couple. Patrick decided on a suit so that he could use his blazer as a coat. Once the sun sat behind the church this evening, the temperatures were sure to drop dramatically. Katie too gowned in her favorite dress. She loved any excuse that allowed her to put on fancy attire.

The couple made sure to recognize the city crew men, and quickly exchanged a Merry Christmas with them. Once pleasantries had been shared, the two made their way to the party at the town center. The yard out in front of the lodge was full of happy children, laughing loudly together as they played in the grass. Patrick loved the sight of kids innocently enjoying their evening as friends, outside of the classroom walls. He and Katie knew each and every child in Ellinwood through their years of Santa and Mrs. Claus. Although the children could never figure out how the Wolf's always seem to know them, they always enjoyed a happy hello from the two souls.

As they entered the large hall, the happy couple was greeted with the sights of holiday decorations and the smells of Christmas Dinner. The aroma of tonight's meal made Patrick's mouth water. The Buffet held all the trimmings. There was a selection of turkey and ham along with fruits and vegetables. But Patrick's eyes grew wide as soon as he noticed that they had made his favorite dessert, cheesecake with cherries on top.

The entire center was decorated with Christmas, thanks to the help of Katie and her sorority sisters, who were honored as this year's hosts. Ribbons and balloons lined the walls of the hall. Paper snowflakes hung from the ceilings and candy cane center pieces were carefully set at every table. Off to the side of the stage sat a large chair that resembled that of a throne meant for a king. Next to the chair stood a makeshift fireplace and a Christmas tree with many gifts underneath the decorated evergreen. Patrick knew right away that Santa would be stopping by tonight to see everyone. With a little regret that he would not be this year's iconic visitor, he did look forward to meeting Santa and wishing him well.

Music and laughter soon filled the room as the town citizens united together to socialize with one another and break bread as a family. Lifelong friendships were catching up on recent events as old acquaintances reunited to tell stories of the days gone by. Large round tables were spread out throughout the hall for everyone's dining enjoyment. Two or three families were placed at each table. As the adults conversed with each other, kids would run from table to table to talk to their friends. The past summer harvests had not been as productive as everyone would have liked, due to the extraordinarily hot season. Nevertheless, everyone was enjoying themselves and absolutely no-one was preoccupied with the devastating harvest, earlier in the year.

Money was indeed tight for the farmers as well as the entire area, but on this evening, the financial hardships were not on the minds of the party-goers. Tonight was the one evening, that everyone came together and openly honored themselves as a community and to spread some Christmas cheer to one another.

Once everyone had arrived at the party, Pastor Al Hysom was invited to give the blessing for the holiday meal. Heads were bowed as the pastor gave thanks. Then after grace was offered, Katie stood up and gave directions to how the buffet line would work. Once the instructions were completed, everyone arose from their seats and filed in line to walk through the buffet. Everyone filled their plates and enjoyed the wonderful food together, not only as friends, but as a community.

Patrick and Katie enjoyed the good conversation with their dinner table neighbors. They spoke about the high school football and basketball teams. This year the football squad did not fare as well as they had hoped; however, the boy's and girl's varsity basketball teams looked very promising. They were hoping for a well-deserved season victory for the kids. Katie and the ladies at the table were happy discussing the school musical that the students put on before Thanksgiving Day. The musical they performed was My Fair Lady. There was so much talent in the cast and the kids worked very hard to make this year's show the best one the town had ever seen. The topic of Patrick playing Santa was not mentioned one time. Everyone had only high respect for the Wolf family, and although this year would bring a little change, they considered Patrick a good friend of the community and held no ill feelings towards him.

As soon as dinner was over, the announcement was made that the time had come to meet across the street, at the park, for some singing before the big lighting moment. Patrick and Katie went over to the coat rack and found their warm jackets. They then made their way across the street to the downtown park. Katie held Patrick's arm as they walked. For Katie, she began to appreciate her newly allotted time with her husband and found new enjoyment in being next to him.

The citizens of Ellinwood, as well as from several of the surrounding communities, were gathering at the Ellinwood city park to celebrate the beginning of the Christmas season together. It was a beautiful evening for the Christmas tree lighting. It was as if the weather seemed to know how important it was to everyone, presenting itself with calm winds so that the celebrators could enjoy the beautiful autumn afternoon. The day had been full of many traditional events, including the dinner they had just completed, leading up to the annual lighting of the town's Christmas tree.

As the crowd gathered, the sun began to fall behind the horizon. The moon then took its turn lighting up the night's wintry sky. It looked as though the moon was dancing on the thick clouds above. Just as the earth's satellite reached its peak point of brightness, the year's first snow of the season began to fall from the heavens. Excitement instantly filled the evening air just as the gentle flakes reached the fingertips of the town's children, and the spirit of Christmas illuminated the hearts of everyone as they began to sing carols in concert.

The local community band and choir led the crowd in an evening of musical festivities. And as the carols began to play, the holiday lights and ornaments along Main Street were lit. The entire downtown shone brightly throughout the park square, transforming Ellinwood into a Christmas wonderland. Children ran and played in the park, excited by the snow. The Christmas season had begun. As for the kids who remained at home for the evening, they too were excited to see the snowfall, pressing their noses against their windows and gazing hypnotically at the trillions of snowflakes falling from the heavens.

Although Patrick was not participating as one of Santa's helpers this year, Santa did make an appearance at the party. The children were excited to see their holiday visitor. They began to cheer loudly as Ole' Saint Nick walked onto the stage and made his way through the band, and up to the very front edge of the platform. He proclaimed the beginning of the season and with a shake of the bells around his wrist, the Christmas tree was turned on, allowing the lights to gleam over the crowd. It towered above the people, and for a moment brought awe to the community and silence to everyone there. The Spirit of Christmas indeed saturated Ellinwood's town square and joy filled the hearts of everyone.

Patrick and Katie stood with their community family, absorbing every ounce of holiday spirit that they could. At the end of the tree lighting ceremony, Katie took Patrick's arm. Deciding not to return to the hall for the dance, they said their goodbyes to all their friends and began to walk back to their car, taking their sweet time as they continued to take in the beautiful evening. The couple had enjoyed every moment of the day together. It was just what they needed to help put aside Patrick's retirement as Santa. It was a beautiful evening and both Patrick and Katie enjoyed themselves immensely, relishing their time with friends and loved ones.

As they approached their vehicle, Patrick began fumbling through his keys to their car. As he searched impatiently, an overall sense of confusion came across him, and he began to feel a sharp pain in his arm. Katie immediately knew that her groom was not well. As he leaned forward onto their car for balance, she tried desperately to comfort him, while at the same time, yelling out for anyone to assist her and her husband. Suddenly, Patrick lost his balance all together and collapsed onto the ground, hitting his head on the pavement. What started out as a beautiful evening, suddenly ended up in chaos as members of the town ran to help Patrick and calm Katie.

It only took moments for the ambulance to arrive as it had been parked at the square for the event. The medics assisted Patrick and Katie into the vehicle and they were rushed to the hospital. Katie held her best friend's hand in an attempt to bring comfort to her husband. As she held him tightly she sang to him, singing his favorite hymns, and praying for him to be well. Being a small town, the hospital was only moments from the park, but before the ambulance could arrive at the emergency room entrance, Patrick went into cardiac arrest. Katie was ordered to sit back as the med crew went to work, doing everything within their power to revive Patrick. Within moments, a husband, a father, a grand-dad, and one of Ellinwood's friendliest citizens was feared dead.

CHAPTER THREE

A Single snowflake fell from the blue sky, gently falling towards the Earth's surface. From out of the heights, the icy crystal glided downward, whimsically following the course of the soft breeze. Upon touching down on the snow below, Patrick appeared.

In what seemed like an instant from the moment he was being attended to, Patrick suddenly found himself in the middle of no-where. The sun was out and there wasn't a single cloud in the sky. All around him stood a forest of trees, thickly spread throughout the rolling hills around him. And beyond the foothills, the giant mountain ranges towered into the clear blue sky above. Patrick was alive and well, but was not quite clear of the recent events that just took place back in Ellinwood. He was a little confused about where he actually was. Just coming into a conscious state, he had a fuzzy memory of the party he and Katie were just attending. He could vaguely remember the Christmas tree lighting ceremony in the park, but the rest of the day was foggy. Patrick had no clue that he had just had a heart attack and that his wife was scared for his life, or that there was an entire community, concerned for his well-being back at home.

Was Patrick dreaming? He really wasn't sure. He looked around and peered through the trees, watching for any sort of clue that would bring his current situation back to light. Yelling into the woods, he listened for a response, but all he got in return was the sound of birds singing throughout the mysterious valley around him.

After a few moments, Patrick finally spotted his first sign of life. A large buck was standing at attention, motionless, watching him. The beautiful animal was guarding what looked like the beginning of a trail that led deeper into the woods. Looking directly into Patrick's eyes, it seemed that the stag was purposely trying to gain his attention. Once the two had successfully acknowledged each other's existence, the deer turned his head and started moving forward, beyond the trail head.

As it made its way, the animal turned back at Patrick again, as if checking to see if he was behind him, and then continued. With a feeling that he should follow his new friend, Patrick felt that he had no choice but to begin the trek forward. As he and the buck hiked down the path, Patrick couldn't help but to notice the beauty of the mountainside, already covered in fresh powdery snow. Although the temperatures were nearly freezing there was no frigid wind, like back at home. Patrick noticed the calmness right away and felt pleasingly comfortable along his walk. He was dressed warmly, wearing a heavy winter coat and had snowshoes tied to his feet, making his hike through the fresh powder quick and easy. Although he knew he was not at home anymore, he felt unusually at home in these woods. And, although he knew he was no-where close to Ellinwood, he felt no fear. Patrick continued on his way, trailing close behind his guide. The only sense he could make of his newly found location was that he was dreaming, and because he was in the middle of a delusion, he had no worries about Katie.

Just as many do during the course of their lives, Patrick had been suffering from joint pains in his knees and lower back. However, finding himself in these isolated woods, Patrick was feeling no pain what-so-ever. In fact, he felt better than he had in years. He felt strong again... youthful even.

As the hike continued, Patrick's dream assumption was confirmed as he passed by a chipmunk, feeding on a stump next to the trail. The chipmunk had a small pile of nuts he had just collected and was placing them in his mouth, making his cheeks puffy. Smiling at the chipmunk, the little creature looked up at Patrick and shrieked at him as if he was speaking to him. And with that, Patrick was convinced that he was, indeed, having a very weird dream. He laughed to himself and kept walking forward, continuing to trail the buck.

After some time hiking through the woods, Patrick began to notice smoke rising from just beyond the trees ahead. The smoke was narrow as if it were coming from a chimney, so Patrick was confident he would find someone to speak with once he reached the nearby farmhouse. A rush of adrenaline came over him and he quickly made his way up the trail, looking vigorously for someone, anyone, to talk to. Still a bit dazed, he wanted to find out why he was here in these mountains and find out what events had led him to this beautiful, yet unusual location.

Once Patrick and the buck crested the top of the hill, Patrick discovered the cottage completely isolated in the valley. Making their way down the final stretch of the trail, Patrick began to grow more and more excited. He wondered what he was about to find. What kind of person or persons would be down there and could they help him get back home.

After arriving at a clearing within the trees, Patrick and his cervidae guide stopped side-by-side for just a moment to look around the lawn before them. Around the entire ranch was a stone fence, trimmed with rustic wood along the top. Within the stone fence stood three buildings, including a barn, stables, and a farm house. Towards the back of the small farm stood a magnificent white barn, soaring well above the other buildings within the estate. There were horses inside the stable as well as reindeer. Animals meant that the owner would have to be nearby. Without hesitation, Patrick passed through the fence's entrance and approached the stable, looking for signs of life. The entire ranch was covered in a blanket of snow, still undisturbed by footprints of any kind. Even the colossal piles of firewood were still covered in white, so Patrick decided that the snow must have been very recent. Over by the barn were several wood carvings of deer, frolicking and leaping through the air. With all the beautiful sculptures, Patrick came to the conclusion that this was the home of a talented artist.

After several moments, the buck lifted his head and stood at attention. It then trotted forward towards the barn. Patrick stayed very close behind. As they approached the large white shed, Patrick heard a faint sound coming from the other side of the building. They made their way closer to the grand wooden hut, and as they approached it, the noise grew louder and clearer until Patrick recognized that the sound he was hearing was indeed human. The voice sounded very much like singing. Once Patrick reached the barn, he looked around attentively for the owner, but could find no-one. Following the sounds of the voice, he looked just beyond the building where he noticed a pond covered in ice, resting just through the trees and down the hill from the area where he was standing. Without hesitation, he quickly and clumsily made his way down the hill to the pond where he finally laid his eyes on a man who was enjoying himself while ice skating, singing happily as he slid across the frozen water. Although he looked friendly enough, Patrick had reservations about coming right out into the open. Unsure if the man would be as friendly as he looked; Patrick kneeled down behind a fallen tree so that he could watch his subject carefully, trying to decide if it was safe to approach. The last thing that he wanted was to be found and considered an unwelcome trespasser on the man's territory.

The man on the skates was a unique looking fellow and seemed to be about Patrick's age, maybe a few years older. He was dressed in mountain clothing that looked Dutch or maybe even Swedish. He was a tall, robust, and very stocky looking gentleman. It was obvious that he was used to life in the mountains and could care for himself very well. With a full head of graying hair and a grayish white beard that was just barely long enough to blow in a breeze, he danced across the lake. It was obvious to Patrick that the man had been out in the mountainous elements for quite some time. His nose and cheeks were bright red as if he had been outside for hours. Breathing heavily, steam rolled out of his mouth with every word sung through his breath. Although a tad unusual, the man's character seemed gentle enough. Patrick decided it was safe to leave his hiding spot and show himself.

A little bit out of breath from his hike in the high altitude environment, Patrick managed to climb back to his feet, approach the edge of the pond, and signal the strange character. He tried desperately to get the gentleman's attention. He waved his hands in the air and attempted hollering to the self-engaged man. But in spite of his best efforts, the freshly fallen snow that covered the ground was absorbing so much of his voice that his shouts dwindled into a mere dull whisper in the air.

Patrick attempted to communicate with all his might. He waved his arms wider and with more animation as he continued to yell out, "Hello there! I say... Hello!"

Finally hearing Patrick's voice, the man turned and saw the stranger standing along the shoreline, waving frantically for his attention. The old man smiled and chuckled to himself. His first impression of Patrick was that he was pure of heart. Finding the humor in Patrick's frustration, the man waved back to him, mimicking his frantic actions. He then gave a friendly wave to show Patrick he had recognized him and was on his way over to meet with him. With a crazy eight like maneuver, the gentleman circled around and began gliding across the ice toward Patrick. He continued singing his song as he drifted forward, and with joy in his heart, the skater continued caroling until the two men finally met face-to-face at the side of the icy rink.

The man reached up and tipped his hat towards Patrick. "Well, hello to you sir! What in the name of Jesus brings you way out here into the middle of nowhere this cold afternoon?"

Patrick was relieved to meet the man. "I was hoping you could give me some directions. I think I'm lost. Somehow, I managed to find your farmstead. I'm sure you're a busy man, but I sure could use your help to find my way back, if you don't mind."

Once again, the man began to hum a little tune. He tilted his head as a silent signal for Patrick to follow him. He slowly skated around the edge of the ice, around towards a landing area where the man had placed his shoes. To Patrick, the old man didn't look as if he was in the least bit concerned or even surprised by his mysterious appearance.

Patrick followed him with urgency. He was no longer sure that this experience was a dream. He had simply never dreamt of anything like this in his life. He walked around the pond with the old man, and while he tried his best to remain patient, he knew that his only hope of going home would be from this stranger.

As they reached an old wooden dock, encased by the ice around it, the man sat down and removed his skates. Breaking from the melody, he pointed to a stone bench, near where Patrick was standing. "If you could be so kind to grab me those boots and bring them to me, I would really appreciate the help."

With a sigh under his breath, Patrick looked over to the bench and went to retrieve the boots that were requested of him. He then stepped onto the dock's platform and approached the location where the unusual gentleman was sitting. With a smile, he handed over the precious galoshes to his new friend.

Very thankful, the man exchanged his skates for the boots. He then placed the leather oxfords onto his feet and laced them tightly. After the boots were secured around his feet, the man began to push himself upright, letting out a loud groan as he stood. Patrick immediately reached out his hand to assist him. Not wanting to come across incapable, the elder gentleman waved him off with pride, and managed to climb back on to his feet unassisted.

The man then dusted himself off and nodded to Patrick, letting out a gentle laugh as he acknowledged his attempt to help. "I can't tell you how good it is to meet you. The name's Christkind, but you can call me Kris. Welcome to my humble homestead!"

Kris reached out his palm towards Patrick. Patrick accepted his gesture by grabbing his hand and the two silently greeted one another.

Kris could see that Patrick was indeed, cold and confused. "First of all, what you need to do is get warm by a hot roaring fire. Come on, let's go inside and relax."

Kris then placed his hand on Patrick's shoulders and the two walked up to the house overlooking the pond. Kris was excited to have Patrick as his guest. "We don't get many visitors way up here at this altitude. I'm glad you found me.

It'll be dark soon, and a winter storm is forecast to arrive this evening. It would've been a shame to get caught up here in its clutches."

The two men reached the house. Kris opened the door for Patrick and invited him to make his way inside. With a few gestures of his hands he instructed Patrick, "Feel free to get out of that gear and make yourself comfortable. Just place your stuff anywhere you wish."

After removing their snowy outerwear, Kris went into the kitchen and quickly turned on the fire to the stove. Looking around for the kettle, he stroked his beard and spoke to himself from under his breath. Finally, his eyes lit up brightly as he found what he was looking for. Kris grabbed the kettle and filled the container with water. Then he placed it on top of the stove and left it to heat.

Looking over to Patrick he could see that his new guest had reservations about making himself cozy in the strange home. Kris did not want Patrick to be uncomfortable. "Please, my friend, sit down near the fire and get yourself warm. It sounds like you and I have a lot to discuss!"

Kris guided Patrick into the living room area so he could relax, continuing to encourage conversation with him. "We probably need to find out just where you came from so we can see about getting you back to your home."

Patrick found a comfortable chair near the fireplace and sat down, letting the heat warm him up. Immediately, Patrick felt relief from the bottom of his feet as he settled in the chair. He then sat back and took a deep breath and allowed his tense hiking muscles to relax.

After a short moment of silence he opened up to his host. "My name is Patrick Wolf. Thank you so much for inviting me in."

Kris smiled. "Ah! A Nobleman! The pleasure is all mine, I assure you."

Patrick looked around the room hoping to see something that might act as a reminder of where he was. The house was very beautiful inside. Knotty pine lined the walls as large tree trunks hovered high overhead, acting as support to the vaulted ceiling. Hanging above them was a giant chandelier of large elk antlers. Tiny lights mingled with the pointy racks as they cascaded downward; dimly and gently bringing illumination to the room. Large flames danced and shouted with glee from within the cobblestone fireplace; bringing warmth to the entire room.

As the sun began to sit for the evening, a rainbow of color shone through a large stained glass work of art, painting the walls with dazzling designs. The inside of the old man's home had a Dutch, Finnish feel to it. Everything inside, from the woodwork to the paintings on the wall, as well as the furniture, felt very European. Over the fireplace was a beautiful wooden train set. The attention given to the craftsmanship of the train was remarkable. Right away, it reminded him of a similar model Patrick once had back in his youth. As he continued to look around, he noticed many woodcarvings around the room of various toys, all which looked as though they were put together with great care and patience.

Patrick picked up a small toy and admired it. "You have some beautiful toy sculptures, Kris. Are you a woodcarver or a toy-maker?"

Sitting down in a chair next to him, Kris leaned over and handed Patrick a mug of hot tea. Looking at all the toys, Kris smiled as memories rushed through his head. "I dabble here and there. That train on the mantel? It was given to me years ago from my teacher. In fact, all the toys have been given to me, over the years, from many friends of mine. All of them true artists of the craft. I cherish each and every one of them."

Kris was excited that his guest took interest, and he was more than happy to share his memories with his newly found friend.

Reaching over to the side table next to him, Kris picked up one of his most honored possessions to show Patrick. "Look here! See this pipe?"

Holding up a simple pipe for Patrick to see, Kris held it in his hands, delicately and with pride. The pipe was long and thin. A vine was carved along the length of the shank, ending at the bowl of the pipe where a beautiful rose was engraved.

Kris held it out for Patrick. "As far as all the carvings I possess, this pipe, I cherish more than anything."

Patrick placed his tea on a table next to him. Then he reached out as Kris delicately placed the homemade pipe into his hands so he could get a better look.

Kris was eager to tell Patrick all about his pipe. "This was also given to me as a gift. My lovely wife gave it to me. It was given to her, a very long time ago, by the wife of my predecessor. It's been said that the legendary Saint Nicholas made this pipe by hand. And for those who possess the pipe, they will receive the eternal gift of joy."

Recognizing what he had just said to his confused guest, Kris chuckled with a little embarrassment. "Well... that's the saying, anyways."

Patrick was, again, amazed at the beautiful artifact. He might not have exactly believed the part of Saint Nicholas, but it was a very impressive story and Patrick could appreciate the artisan-ship of the device. After looking it over, he gently handed it back to Kris. "If it was truly carved by Saint Nick, it would be very old. Have you ever smoked from it?"

Kris laughed as he reminisced to himself. He then held it back up to look it over one last time. "Until recently, I used to enjoy a good smoke from this very pipe, but over the years have found that bad things can come from indulging in it too much, so now I only partake annually. Throughout the year, I spend a lot of my time up north. Whenever I go that direction, I bring it with me. Since the moment I was given this vessel, my life has been full of countless joys. I am a blessed man, indeed."

With a childlike smile, Kris gave the old pipe a kiss and then placed it on the end table. He then looked over to Patrick and leaned over closer to him. He could see Patrick was beginning to dry off and was finally getting warm.

Confident that Patrick was feeling at home, Kris decided to take the opportunity and get down to some business. "Now, my friend, how can I assist you today? Tell me what brings you way up here into my mountain."

Patrick sat up in his chair and put it as simply as he could. "I'm not exactly sure I know what's going on. I think I might be lost, but then again, I might be dreaming. And if I'm dreaming, then that means none of this is real."

Kris chuckled at Patrick's honest response. He leaned back into his seat and then responded. "Do I look like a dream to you? Did that cold air feel like a dream to you? And, does that warm tea taste like a dream to you? You sir, are indeed very exhausted, but I can assure you, I am as real as can be."

Seeing that Patrick was in thought, Kris continued. "Now think, Patrick. What's the last thing you can remember before mysteriously showing up at my home?"

Patrick was trying to recall the moments that led up to his appearance in these mountains but he simply could not retain any sort of time line. "I remember my wife and I were at our little town's Christmas tree lighting celebration, but the rest is all a blur. Then I woke up right here where I found you and your farm. All I know is that I didn't purposely come here; I simply ended up deep within these mountains and don't have a clue as of how. I'm lost and I have no idea how to get back home."

Mr. Christkind smiled. He understood exactly why Patrick was so frustrated. Kris had had a premonition of his appearance as well as the circumstances that led his new guest to his cottage. Patrick's arrival to Kris's home meant that the lives of everyone who had ever known him would no longer be the same. And even though the reasoning behind this meeting was heartbreaking, there was still a great test in front of Patrick. One that could bring a new found life to him and his family, changing them forever. Kris felt sympathy for Patrick's family but was indeed excited to have Patrick as a guest in his home.

Although, Kris knew the importance of Patrick's coming, he did not want to come across as inconsiderate of the situation.

Delicately, Kris prepared Patrick for his mysterious happening. "I understand that you think you are disoriented or that you may feel as if you are stuck in some sort of dream-like state, but Mr. Wolf, you are definitely not lost. You may not completely understand the circumstances that have led you to my home, but you are indeed here for a very important reason, and I am the very person who is responsible for you coming today."

Seeing that Kris had secured his guest's complete attention, he continued softly. "I have been praying for your arrival for some time now. Although I did not know when our meeting would actually take place, I feel that my prayers have been answered with perfect timing. I am so excited that you have been brought to me today, and that we could finally meet."

Kris stood to his feet and walked over to watch the sun set. The towering mountainside began to obstruct the star as it struggled to cast ablaze its final rays of light for the day, and within a matter of moments the entire sky was black.

A word came over Mr. Christkind to get to the point. Dancing around the subject for too long would not help the host or the guest to find trust with one another.

Kris sighed and just let it all out. "You don't have any memory of what has happened to you, and I will not blame you if you should get angry with me for what I am about to say. You see, while you were out celebrating with your wife Katie, you had a heart attack and hit your head pretty hard. An ambulance was sent to help, but you were in very critical condition. At this very moment, Katie is with you. The doctors have done everything possible, so as of now, all anyone can do is to wait."

Patrick was stunned by Kris's news. He could not, and would not give any consideration to this story. He became angered with Mr. Christkind. Kris could see the animosity building up inside of Patrick and knew he would have to act quickly or risk losing him forever. He looked up towards the sky and silently asked for a little help.

Seeing the chaos running through Patrick's head, Kris jumped to a more positive note, in an attempt to divert a possible mental meltdown. "But now, here you are! Right here in my home, very much alive! Earlier, when I got the perception of your passing, I had no doubt that today would be the day we would meet."

Suddenly, Patrick could remember everything, and as the recollections came to him, his visions began to spin as thoughts of his last moments overwhelmed him. He grew scared and he tripped over himself trying to get to his clothes. Shaking heavily, he fumbled to get his boots back on. Kris watched Patrick and knew that he would die if he didn't put a stop to his attempt to leave. As the door opened to the night's elements, Kris had no choice but to meet him at the door and stop his fateful exodus. He threw his muscular arm out in front of Patrick, grabbing the threshold of the doorway, to block Patrick from leaving.

Breathing heavily, Christkind had to stop his new friend. "Where do you think you are going to go, Mr. Wolf? Look out there! I know you are scared, but you will not find Ellinwood this way! God be with your wife, but she is not outside, Patrick! There is absolutely no place for you to go. Please stop!"

With his heart pounding, Patrick stopped and looked out the door into a sea of blackness. His emotions had run away with him but his only reasonable thought was that he needed to get home to Katie.

Kris looked Patrick in the eye. "You've been given a second chance to a new life. Don't give it all up before giving yourself a chance to start. Don't bring this all to an end by doing something you would regret for yourself and for Katie."

The two men stood toe to toe in the doorway. Kris released his clutches from the threshold and reached his hand out, placing it on Patrick's shoulder. Patrick looked at his host in the eyes and could tell that he was not fooling with him in the least. He then looked to the floor underneath them and took a step backwards, allowing Kris to shut the door to the outside. Patrick conceded to the fact that he was not dreaming. When he looked at the face of his strange host he saw complete honesty. He knew the only way to go home would be to hear Mr. Christkind out and consider what he was trying to tell him.

Once his heart stopped racing and he began to settle down, memories of the Christmas tree lighting came back to him. He dropped to his seat and placed his hands on his forehead as he recalled Ellinwood and the entire day's festivities. Katie was so happy to be surrounded by sorority sisters and her family of community friends. Then Patrick evoked having his heart attack and being rushed to the hospital. Thoughts of Katie began to overwhelm him as he recalled the look of sorrow that was on her face. He remembered feeling helpless as he watched Katie cry for him, just before everything faded to black, where he found himself in the mountains.

Patrick began to weep as he thought about Katie. He made a promise to himself, long ago, that he would outlive his wife so that she would never be forced to experience the pain of such a loss, fending all the stresses of life on her own. He felt like he had failed her, without even a hint of warning. Patrick had left her all alone and could not bear it. Patrick needed to return to his home.

Full of a disorientated mixture of rage and sadness, Patrick lashed back. "What do you want from me? Why have you brought me here, and what decision are you going to make about my life? If this is not heaven, send me back. My wife is worried about me and is expecting me home!"

Kris tried his best to respond to Patrick's question with compassion. "I'm not here to place judgment on your life, Patrick. No, I'm not worthy to do such a thing to anyone. I am not here to send you to heaven or hell, nor can I just send you back home. You were, however, selected for great purpose that is well beyond your understanding right now. You are not dead, my friend. You are truly alive, and I hope you will give me the chance to get to know you better and allow me the opportunity to introduce you to a world larger than life."

Seeing that Mr. Wolf's heart was beginning to return to a somewhat normal pace, Kris felt hopeful that the initial hurdle had been passed.

He resumed, but with caution, "It's been a couple days since those final moments you remember up until today. Your body is being kept alive through nothing but a ventilator; however, your brain is no longer functioning as it should. Your wife and children have been told of the possibility that your body could pass if no improvements happen soon. Each one of them has made amends with you and come to terms that the day of your passing is coming. They have said their goodbyes and made their peace with you. A soul such as yours is rare to find any more. That is why you were brought to me."

Kris continued to speak to Patrick. He believed he was finally listening, so he wanted to get everything out into the open without scaring him any further. As he spoke, Kris opened an old storage trunk and pulled out some blankets. As Mr. Christkind continued to explain, he placed the sheets on the couch so that Patrick could rest for the evening.

Christkind smiled humbly towards Patrick in an offering of solace. "I know this has been a lot to take in, but please don't worry about your wife. I can assure you that she will be looked over with care, just like you have done for her. Believe it or not, there is still more for you to accomplish on this earth. You have been sent to me to help me on a very important mission. The last few years have been very trying on me and my family. My wife feels that I could use an assistant so that I can focus on recovering instead of stressing myself to death. You, my new friend, are the only one I would want to help me. You are the only person I know with the kind of heart required for such a task."

Kris wanted Mr. Wolf to be able to sleep well this evening, as the next day was going to bring new changes to the already confused man. He decided it was imperative that his day end on a positive note. He wanted Patrick to be able to find some sort of comfort with his new situation, so that he could get a good night's rest.

Before retiring he looked into his friend's eyes to speak these words of encouragement. "I too am a married man. Because of that I want you to know that I understand your fears right now. I promise you, tonight... I promise that if you help me on my mission, that in return, I will help you. I also pledge to you, as God as my witness, that if you will help me this holiday season, I will return you to Katie. I'll do everything in my power to get you home for Christmas morning."

Returning home was all Patrick wanted to hear. He thought about the agreement that Mr. Christkind had just offered him. He had no way of finding his way home without the help of this man. Although he was not entirely sure on the time line of events that brought him to these mountains, Patrick could find no reason not to believe that what Kris was telling him was the truth.

Kris held out his hand to Patrick and smiled with greater confidence. "Here's to reuniting with your family."

Patrick accepted Kris's offer. And with that, the two shook hands to confirm their newly established partnership together. Patrick then returned a smile to his host. "Amen!"

Kris gave Patrick a few short directions around the house so that he could make himself at home. He then retired to his room for the night. Patrick climbed into his makeshift bed and curled up under the blankets. Looking out through the windows, he could see the moon, glowing brightly, illuminating the mountainous terrain around him. The moon also brought back memories of Patrick and Katie's very first kiss, long ago. He smiled in thought and then began to pray for his Katie. He prayed that she would find a place in her heart to forgive him for leaving her in such an alarming way. He also asked that she would find understanding and patience for him. It had been a very long day and Patrick was exhausted. But before he could even finish his prayer, Patrick's eyes grew heavy, his anxieties began to diminish, and he drifted off to sleep.

CHAPTER FOUR

At dawn's first light, the roosters in the yard began to crow boldly, leading a symphony of nature's music throughout the farm's yard, and echoing throughout the valley. The morning had arrived. Before he could even manage his eyes open, Patrick could hear the delightful sounds of morning. At that very moment, Patrick was happy.

As if on command, the sun rose and began to pierce through the eastern sky, quickly lighting everything under its watch. Patrick sat upright and looked over to the window. Absorbing the endless shapes and colors throughout the valley, it was as if he was looking at a painting. Patrick sat still and appreciated the gift of the moment. During the calm still night, new snow fell from the sky and coated the lawn. Out in the yard, Patrick spied two horses hitched to a unique looking sleigh. He stood up from his makeshift bunk and walked over to the window to look at the team outside. Sleighs were very rare back in Ellinwood as snow was just an occasional visitor to his town. Unsure of his actual location, Patrick could only guess that if there was a sleigh outside, that he must be someplace up in the northern regions.

A loud noise came clanging from the kitchen, breaking Patrick's moment of thought. He looked over quickly into the kitchen, where he found Kris standing with his hand over his mouth. Looking up and locking eyes with Patrick, he began to laugh.

Mr. Christkind chuckled in embarrassment as he greeted Patrick. "Good morning Mr. Wolf! So sorry for the disruption but (waving his hands over the table in presentation) breakfast is served!"

Snickering to himself, Patrick made his way into the dining area and met with Kris where the two sat down to a casual breakfast. Kris had definitely been busy while Patrick slept. The meal looked well made. There was French toast, topped with butter and real maple syrup. To enhance the sweet and savory slices, Kris whipped up some scrambled eggs, accompanied by a dish of thick, juicy bacon. Patrick then spied the coffee. With a smile, he poured himself a full mug of the java and took a sip. His eyes opened widely at the first taste. It had been prepared exactly the way he would have it back in Ellinwood. Kris spared absolutely no detail in order to make his new friend feel at home.

Patrick was so thankful for the thoughtful meal. "This is too much, Mister Christ…"

Kris interrupted his guest. He felt no reason to be addressed so formally. "Please. Just call me Kris. And thank you. I always try to enjoy a large morning meal before tackling the day."

The two jumped in and ate breakfast together. Patrick felt amazingly happy, considering his recent events. He felt at home in Kris's farmstead, which gave him the courage to get to know his host better.

Patrick gazed around the house. "This is a beautiful farm. It feels like a sanctuary everywhere I look. It would be a shame to be the only one here to enjoy it. So you said you were married?"

Kris was relieved that Patrick was beginning to make casual conversation instead of starting the day demanding answers from their previous discussion.

Mr. Christkind loved his wife very much and was all but too happy to discuss her with Patrick. "Everything you see around you was orchestrated through my wife's imagination. She's a wonderful home maker and a talented designer, so between her unique visionaries and my modest carpenter skills, the two of us have created our dream home. I can honestly say that this ranch wasn't just for me or for her, but for the two of us, together."

Patrick loved the beautiful home and its surroundings. He could definitely feel that a woman had help in the making of the farm. There was more to the house than simple walls and appliances. There was laughter and tears shed throughout every corner of the house, and those experiences together were what made up the strong foundation to their home. Patrick then thought of his wife. He thought about the memories he and Katie created over the years, as the two of them built their home together and raised their family, very similar to Kris and his wife.

Following breakfast the two cleaned up the kitchen. After they were finished, Kris handed Patrick some fresh clothing for the day and then headed outdoors to let Patrick get dressed.

Patrick suited up and then made his way outside. The sun continued to climb into the sky allowing Patrick to see across the valley with clarity. Kris was with the hitch team. He had just fed and watered the horses. As they ate, Kris was busy packing the sleigh with the essentials for the day's trip. Patrick met up with them and began petting the horses as his host finished his preparations.

Patrick walked around the rig and admired the artisan skills that went into making such a fine vehicle. The sleigh was entirely hand crafted with the finest hickory and ash woods. He ran his fingers over the hand chiseled designs that ran throughout the entire frame. As he admired the sleigh, Patrick could not help but to think, maybe he had seen a sled just as this, once before. A vision of his childhood rushed back to him at the sight of this magnificent work of art. That vision brought back a fine tuned memory of Christmas Eve from many years ago. Patrick was stunned by this. Why would one of his most memorable childhood Christmas visions be parked in front of him at this very moment? But with a grin, Patrick shook it off as simple fantasy.

Slightly winded from securing the harnesses, Kris pointed out the landscape around them to show it off. "Today's going to be an exciting day, Mr. Wolf. My mountain is not only beautiful, it's magical. Today, I'm going to show you a brand new world!"

The two men climbed into their vehicle and made themselves comfortable. Kris then looked over to his co-pilot with a joke. "Last chance for a potty break!"

Laughing with excitement, Kris shouted to his team, commanding them to go forward. And with a crack of the reins, the two were off on their new adventure together.

As they made their way out of the yard and onto a snow covered road, Patrick could not help but to be taken back by the beauty surrounding him. Animals were abundant here and they were not afraid to share the land with Patrick and Mr. Christkind. As they moved deeper into the woods, the men enjoyed overlooking the valleys as they appeared between the openings of the trees. The scenery was definitely God's work of art.

Kris felt blessed to be able to spend his down time in these mountains. "I love it here in the hills. It reminds me of Christmas year round. I know every person and nearly every animal that lives in these mountains. It is truly the most beautiful place on earth for me. What do you think of my valley, Mr. Wolf? Does its beauty even come close to that of your home?"

Patrick took a deep breath and he smiled as his thoughts went back to Ellinwood. "Ellinwood is the most beautiful place on Earth. Its charm is uniquely different than that of the mountains, but it is full of beauty, just the same."

Kris knew of Patrick's home town very well. "Oh Yes! Ellinwood seems like the perfect place, indeed! Believe it or not, I've actually been there many times. Mostly, I have visited there for Christmas. The town was always so beautiful and everyone was full of the holiday spirit. And, as for you, if I remember correctly, everyone adored you. You were held a little higher than the average citizen. As I recall, you were their Santa Claus."

Patrick was surprised to hear that Kris had been to Ellinwood. Not many people had ever been to the heart of Kansas, let alone his small home town.

With regret, Patrick thought about his Santa days. "Maybe at one time, but times have changed. No-one cares about that anymore. I no longer know who Santa is, or where he is from, or if anyone else cares about Christmas the way we use to when I was a kid. I've become obsolete as Santa, so I gave it up."

The word "obsolete" was definitely not something that Kris believed. Pulling back on the reins with force, the horses came to a complete stop. Kris stood up and turned his body so he could sit against the dash panel. Scratching his chin, Kris thought about what Patrick just told him. He could not understand what Patrick had just said.

Kris sighed with perplexity. "Are you telling me that a man of your age no longer believes in Christmas? You mean to say that life has taught you absolutely nothing about the importance of that day? You must have been witness to at least fifty Christmases so far! How can you sit there and honestly tell me that you no longer know who Father Christmas is, or know if the rest of the world even cares about the most important day of the year?"

Patrick, a bit stunned at the sudden anger expressed by his companion, sat and thought. He felt as if he was just yelled at by his father, back when he was a child. No-one, aside from his own wife, had raised their voice at him for many years, so Kris's outburst forced Patrick to think about his statement in a way he never had before.

Patrick made a second attempt to say what was on his mind. "Christmas died with the ages. No-one cares about Christmas day anymore. All they care about is who can buy the best gifts, no matter the cost. People are no longer above taking from others to fulfill their own Christmas wants. Now, it's all about the bottom dollar. It's all about taking care of their personal desires. And as for the needs of other people, well, who cares about anyone else as long as you got what you want. It's just not the same as it was meant to be. It's all about the big sale days and whatever else they'll manage to come up with next."

Patrick turned his head and looked deep into the hills as he spoke about it. "A lot has changed from when I was a kid. Christmas used to be a time of celebration, but now it either makes you extremely selfish, or overly depressed. If there really was a Santa Claus, we killed him off by demoting him from saint hood to anti-Christ. Christmas is no more, Old Man! Probably never was. I was just too foolish to believe that such a day could remain as pure as it was meant to be."

As Patrick went on, his voice became louder and louder. The horses became frantic and began to grow restless. They then began to run forward. Kris darted back to his seat as quickly as he could, and tried to manage the spooked horses, but could not seem to bring them to rest.

In the chaos, both men stopped talking and desperately focused on stopping the sleigh. As they rushed forward, Patrick could see that their trail was about to come to an abrupt end. But what was worse, he could see that beyond that trail was a valley that plummeted one hundred feet to a cloud covered death below.

Kris began pulling the reins harder and harder. He decided quickly that if he could not stop the horses, then he would use them to his advantage and harness their strength. Patrick pleaded with Kris to stop the rig, but it was too late. The men, the team of horses, and the sleigh flew off the side of the mountain and began to drop rapidly. And just as soon as they drove off the ledge, lightning began to flash around them, blinding Patrick as they dove into the clouds. Patrick let out a yell, when all of a sudden, he heard a loud thunderous explosion, and everything came to an immediate stop.

As the cloud coverage passed from his eyes, Patrick stood up and looked around. For the second time in as many days, he was not sure where he was. The sky was now black and they were no longer in the valley that surrounded Kris's mountain. Looking over towards Kris, Patrick could see that he had complete control of the horses. He then looked straight forward and saw that they were sailing across a massive desert of snow, heading towards an oasis of light, far ahead of them.

With a stunned look, Patrick turned to Kris. "Where are we?"

Kris laughed and gently grabbed Mr. Wolf, returning him to his seat. "Remember the mission I told you about? The one you agreed to help me with? Welcome to the mission. This is my home. This, Mr. Wolf, is the North Pole!!!"

Patrick looked ahead with shock and awe. The stars in the sky and the lights ahead were more beautiful than anything he had ever seen before. Kris laughed loudly as they raced forward through the evening air. Patrick's mind began to run wild, wondering where they were headed, and fascinated about what was to come.

CHAPTER FIVE

As the sleigh drew closer to the lights and approached the entrance to the city, Patrick looked around in disbelief. At first glance, the town looked like a giant Christmas Village, similar to one he and Katie had in their living room. The entire city was brilliantly lit with Christmas lights. The glow bounced back and forth throughout the snow-packed mountain range that surrounded the city, protecting the town and all of her residents from the sub-zero elements, just beyond the rocky ridges.

Proceeding through the city streets, the men were met with friendly waves from the town's residents. It was obvious to Patrick that everyone knew Kris, which meant that he must have been very important to the villagers. The friendly greetings were a welcoming first impression to Patrick, calming any uncertainties he may have had about his new surroundings. It didn't take long though, for Patrick to begin spotting that many of the local dwellers were very short in stature. Confused, Patrick leaned over for a closer look to see if his eyes were playing games with him; however, there was no illusion. The people were very tiny, and Patrick found humor in seeing little people at the North Pole.

Patrick began to laugh to himself as he inquired about what he was seeing. "Are those elves? Those are elves!"

Kris contagiously began laughing along with Patrick. "For lack of a better term, yes, those are elves. These are my friends!"

The gears in Patrick's head began to turn faster. "Then who are you? It looks like everyone knows you. Are you Santa?"

Patrick felt no shame in asking his pilot if he was Santa. He was in an unusual land, surrounded by unusual people, guided by a most unusual man, so Patrick expected nothing less than a remarkable answer from his new partner.

Kris looked over to the child-like Patrick and introduced him to his new home. "Welcome to the North Pole, my friend. Yes, here at the North Pole, I am also known as Santa."

Patrick could not understand why, but he actually believed what Kris had said to him. Overwhelmed with joy, Patrick stood to his feet, raised his hands in victory, and shouted with excitement.

Patrick's voice echoed through the streets. "It's real! It's really, really, real! Thank you Jesus! Hello North Pole!"

Patrick's child-like laughter was like music to Kris's ears, and soon, he too could not contain his happiness. Kris began to celebrate with Patrick as they glided through the streets.

Just like he did when he was a child, Patrick absorbed the views that surrounded him. Never in his wildest dreams did he imagine that the North Pole was such a beautiful place. Each house and building in the village had a brilliantly lit Christmas tree in the front lawn. Large decorations hung within the trees and lights twinkled and danced throughout every branch and pine needle. The elves spared no expense to make sure their homes and work places were equally decorated with the festive lights.

Deep in the protective arms of the mountains, the millions of colored lights managed to bring additional warmth to the town, allowing the residents to live comfortably in its elements.

Continuing down the streets, the elves continued to wave with excitement, saying hello to Santa and his guest as they rode by. The wonderful sounds of bells and music changed from street to street and sometimes Patrick could hear the multiplicity of sounds mingling together, ringing throughout the mountain valley like Christmas perfection.

The magic of the North Pole left no doubt with Patrick of its existence. As they entered the center of the village, Patrick saw a large tree, unlike any other he had seen before. The tree was beautifully decorated, and the lights illuminated the very heart of town. It was obvious to Patrick that this tree was something special.

Patrick was frozen in awe. "That's one beautiful Christmas tree."

Kris smiled at the beauty of the tree as they pulled up to have a look. Although Kris was no stranger to the city's most important center piece, each time he laid eyes on its brilliance, the moment always felt like the first time ever, filling him with gratitude.

Kris looked over at the tree in agreement. "Yes, yes... it's extremely beautiful."

Showing off the many features of the tree, Kris explained to Patrick. "This is the Tree of Life. Every Christmas tree in the world is an important representation of this very tree. Here's a little known fact. This tree helps bring the magic of Christmas to life. It was a gift to us from someone very special."

From under the tree, the men noticed a family of deer, appearing into the lights, enjoying the cool air of the evening. A baby fawn walked up to the wagon. One of the horses recognized the fawn and welcomed him by leaning down to brush noses with him.

Patrick immediately pointed out the deer. "Is that Rudolph?"

Kris smiled at Patrick's newly rediscovered innocence and shook his head. He then climbed down from the sleigh and approached the family of deer, kneeling down beside them in the snow. Patrick watched silently as Kris began feeding the family. He looked down at the fawn that was grazing next to the horses. Patrick was about to climb down from the sleigh, when the baby fawn raised his head and quickly ran behind the tree. The fawn then headed back around to his family where he huddled with them to find protection. Not wanting the deer to run, Patrick remained in his seat and simply enjoyed the moment. He was a guest in this place and did not want to do anything that would disturb its surroundings. Kris climbed back into the sled and took his seat next to Patrick. As he took his place, Kris looked over to see Patrick's uncontrollably perplexed smile. His reactions validated Christkind's decision to bring him here.

Patrick simply could not contain his excitement as he tried to tie all the mysteries together. "We're at the North Pole and you're Santa."

Patrick placed his hands behind his head and leaned back, looking into the evening sky. Under his breath he began voicing his thoughts. "I'm sitting with Santa Claus..."

Kris chuckled and shook his head in acceptance. He then decided to change the subject a bit. "I'm hungry. Are you hungry? Come on, let's go grab something."

Kris gave a gentle command to his horses and they continued on their way. As they drove, Patrick began to anxiously look around again, as if he was trying to find something in particular. With a laugh, Mr. Christkind knew exactly what his new friend was trying to find.

Kris looked straight ahead as they moved down the lane. "Don't you worry about a thing, Mr. Wolf. It's right around the corner!"

As they turned the very corner, Patrick's eyes spotted the renowned building towering above them. Dwarfing any football stadium Patrick had ever laid eyes upon, the North Pole Workshop was larger than life. The men made their way down the main drive to the shop, and as they drew closer to the building, Patrick grew giddy with anticipation.

The dark sky began to glow dimly in the sun as it remained well below the horizon. As the sled reached the workshop, they pulled up to the front entrance and stopped in front of the large doors. Kris parked the sled and the two men hopped off the wagon. Several small men ran out from inside to help manage the sleigh for them. Before going inside, Kris walked over to his team of horses and thanked them both for a job well done. He then looked over to Patrick and the two walked inside the toyshop.

At first glance, Patrick felt like he was in the mountains of Colorado. Kris loved the Rockies, and created a mountainous theme within the entire shop. There was an indoor waterfall with water cascading over boulders, creating the soothing noise of a rushing river. And as the water rushed over the crest of the fall, a wonderful thunderous crash echoed throughout the lobby.

Evergreen trees were placed strategically throughout the room, designing a wondrous picture for Patrick. He and his family loved to visit the mountains, and for Patrick, this felt like a home away from home.

Throughout the workshop, Patrick could see a crowd of tiny elves going about their everyday lives. Some seemed to be casually walking, as others were having intense meetings together, and while others were carrying materials from room to room. Patrick needed no explanation of what they were doing. The tiny people were Santa's elves, working hard building toys for the children of the world. Patrick hadn't felt this kind of joy in decades. Adrenalin began to flow through him with excitement, just as if he was a little boy on Christmas Eve, eagerly awaiting the arrival of Santa Claus. Back at home, throughout the years, Patrick's belief of Santa and the North Pole were tucked deeply away by the guidance of those he knew and loved. His belief of Santa faded from a beautiful reality to a practical state of existence that could only live in one's heart. At least, that's what he had been taught to believe.

To the side of the waterfall was a cabin, and at the top of the front door was a wooden sign that read, "Workshop."

Kris could see that Patrick was very curious about the cabin. "That is the original shop where the elves made all the toys for Christmas. Can you believe how small it was? The first elves didn't have the technology that we have today, but I thank God for humble beginnings."

The men made their way passed the old cabin, where a trail led up a windy path to the top of the waterfall, overlooking the entire workshop. At the summit was a large cliff area to rest and simply enjoy the view. As the men stood, Kris reached over and grabbed a pail of peanuts that was sitting on top of a nearby picnic table. He placed a few nuts in his hand and began to look around him. Within seconds, a chipmunk ran from within the rocks and trees and jumped up to the table bench, near where Patrick was standing. Spying Santa, he then leaped onto the top of the table. Santa laughed and grabbed one of the tiny peanuts, and held it out for his chipmunk friend to take from him. The happy little critter took the morsel and shoved it into his mouth. Once fed, it then dashed away, back to his forest home.

Patrick's mind was swimming with inquest. The revelation of being at the North Pole had opened up a galaxy of questions that he desired answers for. Every Christmas story he had ever heard about, as well as every character he had been told about, Patrick wanted to know more, just as if he was back to his five year old self again.

Kris smiled and looked into Patrick's eyes. Immediately he could see that Patrick was in deep thought. He chuckled with curiosity about the gears that were moving in Patrick's head. He was going to have to get his new friend familiar with his surroundings, or he was going to be asking questions forever.

Kris jumped in and inquired of Patrick. "What's going on in there? What's on your mind?"

Patrick just had to know. "So the elves are real?"

Kris nodded his head. "Yes."

Patrick felt that information of that caliber required more detail. "And they're building toys for the kids?"

Kris was going to have to ride the questions out. "They are."

Hearing Kris's acknowledgment opened up the door to the rest of the Christmas folklore Patrick learned about as a child. Patrick continued to dig. "What about Rudolph and the reindeer games?"

Kris gave Patrick the answer he was hoping for. "Rudolph is here, and I believe you will like him very much. As far as games, I have no idea about any reindeer games they play but they do train every day."

Patrick was still giddy from this new experience. He wanted to know everything he could. "I was seven; I think I gave you some curdled milk. Remember that? Oh! What about all the misfit toys?"

Kris could not maintain Patrick's rapidly changing conversation so he held his hands up and shook them, to grab his pupil's attention. "You get weird when you get confused. Has anyone ever told you that? Look, let me show you around. I assure you, that all your questions will be answered as you get to know us."

The two looked around throughout the entire workshop. Amazed at the sight, Patrick was ready to explore everything around him. He wanted to learn all he could about Christmas at the North Pole, as it was something that everyone at home had all but buried from existence.

Just then, from the tiny trail, food was brought to the gentlemen and they sat at the table. The elves placed a wonderfully prepared meal in front of them, as Kris introduced the servers to Patrick. Food at the North Pole was no less impressive than anything else Patrick had experienced. The two filled their bellies and continued to speak about Christmas. Then, when they were finished, they headed back down to explore.

Kris put his arm around Patrick's shoulder in excitement. "Let's go meet the gang!"

As they made their way around the shop, Patrick was amazed at the sight. Starting with the mail room, Patrick was enthralled as he looked on.

Kris guided Patrick's attention to the room in front of them and began to explain the Christmas process. "Watch as the elves walk over to those large mail boxes and remove the baskets of letters. They are written by children all over the world, telling us what they want for Christmas. The elves place the baskets onto those tiny flat train carts, and then they transport the letters into the registry room where each and every letter is read and verified by the studies."

Patrick was floored to see that the North Pole mail room was for real. He watched and shook his head as he tried to fathom the sheer magnitude of letters that were being delivered.

Kris took Patrick and they walked over to the next room. "After the letter has been read, the child's name and address, along with the child's wish list are entered into the registry and submitted to the toy designers, allowing them to bring up the accurate information about the child's toy, described in their letter."

Crossing the hall to their next point on the tour, Kris made sure not to leave anything out. Patrick was amazed at all the drafting tables that filled the room. Several of the elves sat quietly at their desks drawing toy diagrams, while others were studying the drafts that had been drawn already. Kris and

Patrick walked up to one of the tables, occupied by one of the creative elves. Kris patted his elf on the back and greeted him.

Kris then pointed out what was happening before their very eyes. "The toy designer studies the instructions, paying attention to every detail. From there, he goes through the database, in search of established designs. If the child's toy is unique to the workshop, the designer will draft an official blue print for the toy and prepare it for production. Also, the designer will enter the blue print into the workshop database, helping to streamline the production process, should any other children wish for this same toy in the future."

Kris then stood on his tip toes and pointed to the back of the room. "Once the blue print is entered into the system, the toy-makers receive the design and go to work, building the perfect toy, exactly to specs, for each and every child."

Patrick was very excited to see the operations happening before his very eyes. Looking around to see if anyone was watching, he pinched himself to make sure he was truly awake and that this magical place was indeed real.

Kris wanted to make sure that Patrick understood why their process was so successful. Remembering that his guest had been depressed about life at home, Kris wanted to make it very apparent why they can do what they do, year in and year out, without fail. If he could make Patrick understand their focus, he thought that maybe Patrick would bring a little of their magic back home with him and continue that success.

Kris looked Patrick in the eyes and made it very clear to him. "It is important that everyone here at the workshop is working in the department that fits their personal desires, talents, and purpose in life. We only want toys made with a happy heart. This way each and every toy made within our shop is built to perfection and with love for the child of that toy. The one thing we do not want is for a young child to open a present that was created by an elf that had anything but a pure and happy heart at the time of the build."

Patrick loved his years as Santa, but over time he had let the world's beliefs influence his happy heart, causing him to forget the purpose behind his Christmas role.

Kris said farewell to the designer and the two made their way out of the room. Kris didn't want to leave out the true purpose behind the workshop.

Kris took his hand and spanned the entire shop and proclaimed the reason behind their success. "The very first gifts of Christmas were given in adoration and with worship, worthy of a king. That is why we are here. It is our purpose to present that same joy to the world and to continue those blessings that were expressed from the very beginning."

Patrick and Kris continued their tour around the workshop. This evening, Patrick was introduced to a Christmas that previously, he could only imagine. The North Pole was real, and all of its inhabitants were very much alive. For the first time in a decade's worth of time, Patrick saw Christmas in a new light. He wanted very much to return this revelation back home to Ellinwood, and bring this magical feeling to everyone he knew.

Patrick was amazed to see the thousands of toys racing along the roller coaster of conveyors throughout the workshop, making their way to the gift wrapping department. Without a moment of haste, the toys were taken from the conveyor and over to the tables where massive roles of wrapping paper were used to disguise the toys. The elves took each toy and wrapped them with precision. Once complete, the elves topped the packages with ribbon and hand written tags, letting each child know that their present was made just for them.

After Kris had given Patrick his orientation of the workshop, the two stopped and looked around where they had just visited. Everyone and everything working within the colossal building worked flawlessly like a well-oiled machine.

Kris then tried to sum up everything Patrick had just witnessed. "Well, my friend. In a nutshell, this is how we do it. After all of this hard work, it comes down to the big ride. On Christmas Eve, I take every single package and deliver them to their final stops. And with the grace of God, every kid will have a gift waiting for them on Christmas morning. Then, we take a well-deserved rest and do it all over again, for next year."

As belief sat in, Patrick accepted that the workshop was very real and that the operations were successful by staying true to their values. He contemplated everything for a bit and thought to himself.

Then Patrick turned to Kris and asked. "Why am I here then? I can't see how you could benefit from anything I would have to offer you."

Patrick was humbled by what he had just seen. He was overwhelmed with his new found knowledge and could not fathom how he could make a difference in something already so enormously perfected. His Santa role in Ellinwood seemed so minimal compared to what was being accomplished at the workshop.

Kris crossed his arms and responded. "All of our unique purposes are given to us, just a little at a time. Your purpose here is to start with step number one. Then on to step two, and then three, and four, and then the next, and the next, until one day soon... you have fulfilled your purpose here."

And with a snap of Kris's finger, a large door opened up in front of them and a light beamed brightly onto two shiny snowmobiles. Kris laughed and held up a set of keys. He dangled them in front of Patrick, and then dropped them. Patrick immediately held out his hand and caught the keys, clutching them in his grip. The two men jumped onto their vehicles, and started their engines, revving the throttles.

Kris shouted out to Patrick. "Follow me!"

Patrick nodded his head and shouted "HO!" and the kid-like men raced away from the building, back into the darkness. As they raced, all the city lights around them diminished, leaving only the headlights from their snow mobiles to lead the way. The men continued forward as a dim light began to appear over the horizon.

Kris leaned over and yelled out a challenge to his opponent. "Last one to that light up there has to clean the reindeer stables!"

Patrick raised his hand and gave Kris the thumbs up. "Ha! You're on!"

Approaching the light, stars bursting from the surrounding ice in the atmosphere, the racers suddenly found themselves in a dark village where many of the elves called home. The men slowed to a gentle cruise, throttling down in order not to disturb any of the residents within the neighborhood. They continued forward, entering a small park and up to the edge of a small fishing pond, covered in a sheet of ice. The men came to a stop and shut down their machines.

Leaving their snowmobiles, the men walked side-by-side to a bridge that arched over the lake, leading over to a tiny island in the center.

Patrick stopped and leaned over the side of the bridge, looking over towards the lights of the town, bouncing off the ice below. The lights of the town were brilliant and spread high into the atmosphere, illuminating the way for a galaxy of falling snowflakes, gently descending from the clouds above.

Patrick loved this location. He looked down below, into the nightly shadows and then looked up again as he spotted something out in front of him that brought a smile to his face.

Patrick pointed it out to Kris. "This reminds me of home. You know, we had a church across the way, similar to the one just over there."

Patrick pointed to a dimly lit church building beyond the park from where Kris and Patrick stood. Patrick just looked forward as a thought came to mind. This very spot reminded him of Ellinwood. For the first time in a couple days, he felt at peace.

Patrick filled Kris in on what he was thinking about. "When we were kids, my brother and sisters and I use to make our way over to a park, just like this, after the Wednesday evening church services. If we were lucky enough and the timing was just right, we would spy a single ice skater, racing around the ice, appearing from the dark scene, coming around the edge of the pond, and then disappearing back into the black air. Only our imagination could fill in the story of where the skater went. And just when we thought he was gone, he would re-appear back into the light again, racing past us. I remember wanting to be like that skater, brave enough to enjoy his passion with very little light, and having the faith to trust that the ice would have the strength to hold him. The man seemed perfectly content to enjoy the evening, on the ice, in solitude."

As Patrick continued, a dark object appeared below the two from under the bridge where they stood. Catching their eye, their attention on the lights shattered as they quickly looked down to see an image of a skater, just like the one Patrick had just spoken of, gliding elegantly from under their platform and across the glowing ice in front of them. Like a fast moving race car, the silhouetted individual screamed like a rushing wind across the glassy surface and around the edge of the track, on around back into the night. It was just like the childhood memory Patrick had just described, way back in his day.

Kris had a brilliant idea. "Come on Patrick. Let's join him!"

Patrick had not considered ice skating since he was a young man. When he was younger, Patrick was fearless and his imagination ran wild, creating a desire to push the limits on life. But over the years and after decades of life failed experiences, Patrick had built a wall around himself, shutting out his dreams, leaving only the assurances of life, secured by never going outside of his mental construct.

Kris could feel Patrick trying to rebuild that wall around him. He was not going to let Patrick miss out on any more of life's experiences. If he was going to help his friend, he was going to have to lead by example and get Patrick to re-engage with life again.

Kris interrupted Patrick's doubt with a word. "No! Don't let yourself fall back to where you were. Get out on that ice and tear down your hesitation. You may find a treasure greater than gold, simply by taking a chance on your destiny. Only you can reach out and surpass your fears."

Kris wanted nothing more than to help him regain a curiosity of the unknown. With encouragement in his voice, Kris once again laid down a challenge. "What do you say sir? Is today the day you stop letting those fears dictate to you and let the true blessings of life come upon you? Put on those skates and let's have some fun."

Patrick heard what Kris had said. He knew that Kris was correct and trusted him enough to let those words sink in. With a grin, the two made their way down the bridge and to the pond below. Lacing the skates, Kris was the first onto the ice. Kris loved skating and could not resist making his way out to do a few crazy eight like spins.

Patrick slowly made his way forward, meeting Kris. Kris took his arm to steady his friend and then guided him forward, across the frozen water. Taking it steady, helping Patrick to find his balance, Kris gradually began to pick up speed until they were gliding around the lake at a nice cruise. Feeling that Patrick had found his footing, Kris released his arm and let Patrick pilot himself around the icy surface.

Patrick's eyes grew wide as he looked up at Kris in amazement. "Hey, I got it! This is amazing! I'm surprised my ankles are holding up so well."

Kris laughed in support and nodded his head in agreement. "You're a natural!"

Continuing around the corner, the dark skater that Patrick and Kris had been watching went speeding by them, racing out in front of them. He then shot around the pond, back into the darkness.

Feeling young again, Patrick suddenly felt the desire to catch the skater. He dug his blades into the ice and pushed himself forward, picking up speed. The two men found themselves in a sprint. As they raced, Patrick let go of his inhibitions and just enjoyed the moment. The faster he moved, the more the world around him began the blur and glare from his swift forward motion. Looking around, he saw that he had left Kris behind as he flew solo across the ice. Patrick could see the lone skater appearing from the darkness as he made his way closer to him, until he was skating alongside of the man. Looking over to the skater, he smiled over to him, finally getting a view of him after a lifetime of curiosity.

Patrick recognized the skater. It was Mr. Schroeder from his elementary days. The world around him suddenly returned to crystal clarity, and Patrick found himself back in Ellinwood. Mr. Schroeder looked over to Patrick and returned the smile. As the two passed under the dark bridge and made their way out to the open ice, they raced around the edge of the pond, circling back around to the other side of the rink. Patrick caught an image on the side of the lake. Looking over, he noticed four children standing and watching as the men flew across the ice. Patrick recognized one of the children as his little sister. At that moment, Patrick noticed that he was back to the very moment that he was reminiscing about just moments before.

Schroeder tipped his hat to Patrick and then left him behind, disappearing into the dark air on the other side of the lake. Patrick slowed down and looked around. He was home and was reliving a moment he had always cherished in his heart. He approached the dark side of the pond and smiled as his childlike-self began to enter him. Memories from that evening were fresh in his mind, just as if he were living back at that moment. It was an amazing experience. Coming back around the pond, Patrick saw Kris slowly making his way along the frozen surface. Patrick caught up with him and the two simply continued forward for several moments. No words were spoken. Kris understood what Patrick was feeling and did not want to disturb the moment. Kris looked over to Patrick and caught him wiping tears of joy from his eyes. Quietly, they continued on.

After several minutes, the men noticed the young children making their way back to the church across the street, back to where their parents were waiting on them. As they walked,

Patrick tried to make out the parents, but they were too far away to be recognized.

After watching the children, Kris and Patrick returned to the side of the pond where they removed the skates and hopped back onto the snowmobiles.

Kris thought about it for a moment. After the day they had spent together, Kris knew deep down inside that Patrick was going to fit in well here.

Kris looked over to Patrick. "Welcome to the North Pole. This place can be magical at times."

Patrick was happy. He felt at home. "I remember those years of my childhood well. Christmas time back then was always the most wonderful time of the entire year."

Kris inquired of Patrick. "You mean, back in the days when anything was possible during the Christmas season, right?"

Patrick thought about that for a moment and then agreed with Kris. The moment he had just relived was back in a day when Christmas was cherished and all of its mysteries were possible.

Putting on his helmet, Kris reminded Patrick of his purpose at the North Pole. "Remember, you are here to find that magic of Christmas again. Not only for yourself but for the sake of everyone you know. Tomorrow, we start training for Christmas Eve. Remember the years when Christmas was most remarkable to you and harness those times. For what you are about to experience will seem impossible to the mind of a person who has forgotten his childhood. You will need to believe in the magic of Christmas."

Patrick nodded his head. He was aware of what he needed to do. "Where are we off to now?"

Kris was spent for the day. The past twenty-four hours had been a real roller coaster. "Let's head Home. It's been a long day. Let's get you to the ranch and get some sleep. Tomorrow will be here soon enough. I need you to be well rested, because we have a lot to do, and Christmas is right around the corner."

After the magical moment, the two made their way from the park and back into the darkness, towards the ranch, ending a beautifully magical day.

CHAPTER SIX

P atrick laid in his bed; sound asleep, with the blankets pulled over his head, covering him completely. It had been a good day for Patrick and the rest was well deserved. Patrick's last thoughts of the day were ones of hope and expectation of things to come. He actually fell asleep with dreams of Katie, and the belief that he would see his family again.

The sunrise at the North Pole was unlike that of what Patrick was familiar with, almost, other worldly, from Ellinwood. During winter time at the North Pole, day was night and night was night. Yet there was a beauty to all the blackness. Patrick's vision of Christmas Eve, back at home, seemed to be the everyday normal at the North Pole during the wintry months. Everything black was illuminated by lights. Lights of countless colors brought new life to a land where very little natural light of its own was produced for extended periods of time. The lights brought life and warmness to the North Pole as well as a feeling of magic to the community.

From out of his dead sleep, Patrick heard a voice. "Good morning, my friend."

Startled by the voice, Patrick sat up in his bed, with the sheets still clinging over his face. With a guilty grin, Kris stood back, remembering that Patrick was not used to being at the North Pole, nor was he used to waking up to the sound of a grown man in his room. Kris could not resist the ghostly sight before him and began to chuckle. Patrick turned his head towards the sound of Kris's voice, still trying to wake up.

Kris began to laugh and then pulled the blankets from Patrick's head. "Good morning, Mr. Wolf."

Patrick wiped his eyes and scratched his head and looked at Kris. Kris made every attempt not to laugh as he found humor in his new friend.

With a guilty grin, Kris greeted his friend. "It's going to be a good day, indeed. Welcome to your first day of training."

Kris snickered as he turned and left the room, trying to keep his laughter under his breath. Patrick watched as Kris made his exit, and then he looked around trying to gain awareness. Looking towards a dim lit lantern, he spotted a photo of Santa and Mrs. Claus. Instantly, Patrick smiled, remembering exactly where he was. He was excited to tackle the day that awaited him. Patrick threw the covers off of himself and jumped from the bed. He was excited to see what new mysteries awaited him.

With zest, Patrick opened the door to his room and found his way to where Kris was waiting for him. Next to Kris was a beautiful lady. Kris introduced Patrick to his wife, Pinky. Her smile was full of joy and brought a sense of sanctuary to Patrick. Patrick reached out to shake Pinky's hand; but instead, was pulled in and given a warm hug as if he were a lifetime friend. Patrick accepted Pinky's gesture and smiled.

Pinky's voice was so happy and welcoming. "Santa has told me so much about you. It is so nice that we could finally meet. Everyone is excited that you have come to be with us this year. The buzz is all over the workshop. We know you will be a great addition to our family and will help us make this Christmas the best one yet."

Pinky handed the two gentlemen a bag full of breakfast food and sent them on their way, blessing them and commanding them to have a wonderful day. Kris then escorted his friend out of the house to show him the ranch. However, before getting too serious about training, he first wanted to introduce him to some of his friends.

As they made their way across the yard to the buildings on the other side, the two ate their breakfast that Pinky was so kind to make for them. Reaching what looked like a stable;

Kris extended his hands and unlatched the gate that surrounded the building.

In a quiet voice, Kris explained to Patrick the purpose for this stop. He knew that this was going to be a much welcomed surprise for Mr. Wolf. "I want you to meet some of my friends. Without them, Christmas just wouldn't be the same."

Opening the doors to the stable, Kris smiled as the gate glided along the rails, allowing the lights from within the stable to spring from the inside and illuminate the presence of an eager Patrick. The swooshing sound of the entrance doors stirred the inhabitants inside the stable. Instantly, several heads began popping up to see who had come to see them.

Upon seeing the happy faces that were looking back at the men, Patrick smiled, and was washed over with great joy.

Inside the stables, Santa's team of reindeer came out from their quarters to be greeted by Kris and his new friend. They lined up and stood at attention. The team of caribou highly respected Kris. And for Kris, he felt honored to have his hoofed friends. The group had experienced the world together and had an unbreakable bond between them, similar to that of a warrior and his animal partner. The camaraderie within the group was more than just man and animal. Within this small group, everyone was family.

Patrick was enthralled at the very sight. They were not the tiny reindeer that he had envisioned them to be as a child. He had always expected the animals to be similar to that of the white tailed breeds back in Ellinwood, or delicate like the cartoons and storybooks he had been raised on. Patrick had never fathomed what stood before him. Santa's team of caribou was mighty in stature. They were larger than life. The team of deer towered in size, exceeding their cousins, the great elk, and nearing the size of moose. Their shiny coats of fur glistened from the stable lights, revealing every extruding muscle in their bodies. They were solid and bold like soldiers.

Their antlers looked healthy and strong enough to help shield them from danger, or to be used as tools, or even weapons.

These caribou were not intended to be bred for farm use or raised as livestock. This team of animals was raised with the strict purpose of flying Santa around the world, withstanding extreme circumstances along the way. A mission that, just days ago, Patrick thought impossible.

Mr. Christkind was proud of his team. When in their presence, Kris stood just a little taller, knowing just how influential they were to Christmas. They had all been through a lot together, and Kris respected them very much.

Kris held his hands out with pride, showing off his team. "Allow me to introduce to you, my squadron of traveling companions."

Kris walked up to the front of the line and announced each deer by name, one at a time, to Patrick. "First, meet my

Wheel Team, Dasher and Dancer. Dasher and Dancer hold the rear of the team. They are the largest deer of the entire squad. After all, their role will be to hold up the weight of the sleigh, the packages, and even us, as we make our launches and climb in altitude. I have very high expectations of these two. They will be keeping the sleigh nice and level, keeping us from crashing to the surface of the Earth, if you know what I mean."

Patrick smiled and nodded to both Dasher and Dancer, and just like a soldier to his commanding officer, the two returned the greeting, as a respectful salute to their new friend and squad member.

Kris made his way down the line and continued with the introductions. "Next, our Team Deer. Meet Prancer, Vixen, Comet, and Cupid. They will be responsible for maintaining the speed and velocity of the sled. These four deer are our brawny ones. It's a very demanding role and will require every ounce of strength from the four of them, to accomplish such a task."

In unison, the four deer gave their recognition to Kris and Patrick, as they moved down the line. When Patrick first gave thought to the size of the deer, he felt very uncertain in their presence. However, although they were all great beasts, when he looked in their eyes he saw kindness in their hearts, and his insecurities finally subsided.

With a firm tap, Kris patted the shoulders of the next Caribou in line. "Here we have Donner and Blitzen. These two will be making up our Swing team. Don and Blitz are the ones that will help me steer this rig around some very tight corners. They are our most athletic deer, and can go all night long without rest."

Looking over to the final team member, Kris smiled brightly as he knew that this was who Patrick had hoped to meet the most. "Lastly, but absolutely not least in any way, meet Rudolf, our team's Lead Deer. You've heard the stories of Rudolf and yes, he comes fully equipped with that supernatural red nose. On Christmas Eve, he will be the one to guide our sleigh and create the pace for our journey."

Kris leaned in to Patrick and nudged him with a whisper. "Rudolf is the brains of this outfit, but don't tell the others."

Patrick reached out and placed his hand on Rudolf's shoulder. He was amazed at the shear muscle that he and each of the reindeer possessed. And as he looked the mighty beast over, Rudolf's nose began to shine. Patrick was amazed to see such a sight.

Kris was proud of his team. They had been through a lot together. "Well, this is it, the famous unit of reindeer that will be joining us on Christmas Eve. I am honored to be on the same team as this group of fellows."

Kris gave the order for the deer to return to their quarters. Each of the caribou let down their towering attention and relaxed as they gently made their way back to their private areas.

Looking around the stable room, Patrick noticed the gear, that the team would be wearing, hanging on the walls. Amazed, Patrick walked over for a closer look. The harnesses looked heavy and impenetrable, like that of an armored modern day soldier. Patrick's impression of the caribou was no longer that of simple drivers that flew Santa around the big-wide-world to deliver presents to the children, as they sang "Here Comes Santa Clause." Patrick had just met a squadron of great warriors whose sole purpose was to transport Santa on his mission. This very sight brought new revelation to Patrick that the flight around the earth was going to be even tougher and more dangerous than he had ever considered.

After meeting the deer, Kris and Patrick were met by Mr. John Dreiling, the lead rancher and Kris's most trusted friend and assistant. Kris reached out and shook John's hand and wished him a good morning. He then took his free hand and placed it on Dreiling's shoulder and introduced him to Patrick. Although Patrick was happy to meet Mr. Dreiling, John was even more so, as he met with Patrick. John had worked with Kris for several decades and over that time, John had been there to witness Kris's slow decline in strength and stamina from the pressures of flying around the world each year. Although Kris had many years within him still, John was happy to see that Kris had finally decided to bring Patrick on to assist him for this year's Christmas ride.

After introductions, Mr. Dreiling took the men to show them their new training facility. Kris was not aware that the construction had been completed, so he was very excited, along with Patrick, to see what Mr. Dreiling had in store for them. John lit three lanterns and handed one to Patrick and Kris, and the three set out into the twilight.

Walking just over to the edge of the ranch and looking over the shallow valley below. John pointed downward to a mass of trees. "It's right down there! Beyond those trees is where you will be spending the next few weeks, training with me."

Patrick was suddenly hit by those words Mr. Dreiling just spoke. Seeing the North Pole was amazing, but when he realized he was going to be training for the next few weeks it became apparent to him that he was now, officially part of the Christmas to come. That, what he was about to endure, was going to change his life forever. Butterflies began to fill his gut and although Patrick was excited, he was now nervous and could feel the pressures of succeeding overwhelming him.

Kris looked at Patrick. He could sense that Patrick was feeling nervous and decided that there was no time to let those feelings of reservation build up. Kris decided that the time was either now or never. "What do you say, men? Race you to the bottom!"

With that, the three gentlemen set out downward, toward the wooden area that awaited them. Although the men were no longer living in their youthful bodies, they were still capable of the vigorous activities that were once included in their everyday lives, just thirty and forty years ago.

Patrick was the first one to reach the front line of the trees; however, both Kris and John were close behind him. The three men paused to catch their breath and began to laugh. Although they all did well on their descent through the snow, and even though they were able to prove to each other that they were not over the hill, it was obvious that they were not ready for Christmas quite yet. There was going to be no time to waste. They had only three weeks to get into enough shape to deliver the presents to every child that inhabited the earth. There was no waiting for tomorrow. Today was the day.

The men began their trek through the dark forest, holding their lanterns high for a better view. In no time at all, lights began to twinkle through the group of trees until they were close enough to see the lights with clarity, welcoming the men as they reached the end of the shelter belt. They stopped and looked in amazement. Before them stood a three story barn where they were going to spend their time in preparations for the upcoming holiday.

The building was decorated with Christmas lights mimicking that of the homes Patrick was accustomed to back in the lower forty-eight states, and back in Ellinwood. The barn also had its touch of decorations. It was calming to Patrick and felt just like home. Suddenly, the stillness of the morning was attacked by a gust of strong wind and snow, also similar to the wintry conditions back at home. All three men wrapped their arms around themselves for warmth.

Kris tried to look up to John without freezing his face. "Well, I can now see why you chose this location, Mr. Dreiling!"

If the men were going to get the most from John Dreiling's training, they were going to have to be exposed to, not only the calmness of Christmas but the extreme harshness that they would have to inevitably endure on their journey.

John moved forward, waving towards the others, motioning to them to follow him. They quickly made their way towards the barn to get out of the vicious winds and into a warmer location. Reaching the wooden structure, John quickly managed to unlatch the lock to the barn door and pull it open. The men raced inside and helped John close the barrier behind them. Amazingly, just as soon as the protective barn doors were shut, the wind came to a stop, leaving the forest opening quiet once again.

The glow of the lanterns bounced off the many nearby walls, but the lights quickly diminished into the darkness, just a few feet beyond. Both Patrick and Kris were full of wonderment of what lay in store for them. After a moment of looking around into the nothingness, bright lights suddenly began to shine throughout the barn and all of their questions were quickly answered.

John had been very busy in Kris's absence down south. He had created an old school training environment for Kris and Patrick that would guarantee success on their journey.

Looking around the room, everything the men would need to prepare for their conditioning was gathered inside the large housing. Patrick immediately spied the free weights along with machines to help him work on his strength. During his teenage years, weight lifting was Patrick's favorite pass time, along with playing football and basketball. Lifting weights was something that Patrick was familiar with, so he was very excited to see that they would be part of their strength training regimen.

One of the barn's walls was covered with a trail of simulated rocks, starting at the ground and leading up to a loft above them. To enhance the big climbing wall, there were several smaller walls draped with ropes, also designed for climbing. At a glance, Patrick and Kris could see that there was an entire obstacle course that was just waiting for them to take advantage of. Although Kris had been doing this for a very long time, he was indeed taken back by the thought of training in this barn. John had promised him a newer and better suited building and was true to his word. Even though Kris was happy with the results, he was very unsure of his abilities. Patrick too was nervous but kept telling himself that the reason he was here was because Kris believed in him. Keeping that in mind, he was at least open to giving the next three weeks the best effort he could rally.

The entire building was full of equipment that the men were familiar with; however, there was one spot that they were unsure about. Kris pointed towards the very center of the barn and questioned what was there. John smiled and flipped on one more set of lights so that the men could see what occupied the heart of the facility.

John was quite proud of his new building and was excited to train the men in his gym: "Gentlemen, let me introduce you to the Octagon."

Both Patrick and Kris stood in wonder of the cage that stood before them. They both knew what an octagon was used for, but confused on how this contraption was going to assist them in training for Christmas Eve. The two looked to John for a boost in guidance.

John held up his hands and then clinched them tightly. "We're going to learn Hand-to-hand combat, my friends. Santa, you almost lost your life to that professional Muay Thai fighter in Sezzadio Italy, last Christmas. Remember, little Antonio's father? Well, this year Antonio is asking for a new bike so we're going to update our combat training, and give you some basic defense skills."

Patrick had never put any thought into Santa's Christmas Eve journey. Until now, he couldn't imagine his trip being anything more than jumping down the chimney and putting toys under the tree. To learn about the evils of little Antonio's dad, was new and a bit disturbing to Patrick.

Patrick nervously spoke his feelings. "I guess the North Pole is more than just toys, wrapping paper, and tape, huh?"

Kris just laughed; as he too used to think the Christmas process was as simple as that. "If there is one thing I have learned over the years, is that our mission here was not constructed for our own glory but for God's. I've also learned that our mission, up here in our little spot of the world, will never be understood by the rest of the people down below. This can sometimes create confliction for the folks whose mission is to protect their families from intruders."

Patrick was now nervous. "So when do we start?"

Kris didn't give it a second's thought. "Right now's a good a time as ever!"

With a grin, John clapped his hands together as loudly as he could. "Well then, let's get moving! Dressing rooms are off to the left."

Everyone went to their rooms, found their workout uniforms, and prepared for boot camp. Once dressed, they returned to the middle of the barn with John, where everyone was ready.

John walked over to the side of the room and put his hands on the latch of the large barn door, announcing the beginning of training. "Merry Christmas, gentlemen! Let's go!"

The three men swung open the barn doors and made their way back out into the snowy elements. Running through a foot of fresh snow, the men made their way, beyond the barn yard, and into the open wilderness where the elements were frigid and deadly.

If Kris was going to get home to his wife on Christmas Eve he was going to have to put every ounce of his heart into making sure the trip was successful. Patrick's motivation was to go home. Like warriors, Patrick was going to have to push himself beyond his capabilities and put his unit first. If they acted as a team, everyone would reap the rewards of a job well done. For Patrick, his reward would be Katie and his family.

Immediately, like the force of a cinder block hitting his chest, Patrick felt the cold winds strike him, trying to break Patrick and make him give up. John, seeing the look of doubt in Patrick's eyes, made sure to take his mind off the cold, by yelling commands at him, pushing him harder with as loud of a voice as he could muster.

John, although a very kind soul, knew the importance of Patrick's visit to the North Pole. He had spent his life, assisting Kris and making sure he was the best Santa the world had ever known, but over the last few years, it was apparent that Kris was no longer in the prime of his life and was going to need a little more help. Patrick's heart attack was the miracle that Kris needed to help him this Christmas. If Patrick was to fail at helping Kris succeed, then he too, would fail. Failure would mean that for the first time in Christmas history, the children of the world would wake up on Christmas morning with no gift, creating a snowball effect of disbelief in Santa. John had dedicated his life to the mission of Christmas, and he had prayed very hard for wisdom to help Kris. He was happy that Patrick had come to the North Pole, and he was going to do everything in his might to help Patrick find success in this year's mission.

John's naturally calm voice was going to have to be loud and powerful in order to train the men and get them acclimated to the chaos that awaited them.

The men pushed forward, against the arctic winds. Whenever any of the three men began to fall behind, the other two were there to push their team mate and give encouragement. And just when Patrick and Kris thought they had reached the end of their first trial and were ready to turn around, John pointed to the top of the hill, in front of them, and shouted for them to climb it. Without a moments rest, Patrick and Kris started up the hill, falling onto all fours for strength. The climb was too much for just their legs alone.

The men quickly learned that if they were going to make the summit, they were going to have to rely on each other to get there. This Christmas was going to be a team effort and if one were to fail so was the other. Although both Patrick and Kris had experienced hardships in the past, neither man was accustomed to accepting failure. The two were going to have to become like brothers and put each other first in order to succeed on Christmas Eve.

Upon reaching the top of the hill, Patrick collapsed and laid flat on the ground. Kris, also winded, was not new to the cross training regimens. He reached down and grabbed the back of Patrick's coat between the shoulder blades and pulled, helping Patrick get back to his feet. Patrick had not used his legs in such a demanding way for many years, and even though he was used to going to the gym to keep fit, he was simply not prepared for the type of conditioning that was going to be demanded of him.

Patrick struggled to get to his feet. His ankles were in pain and his calves were nearly ready to implode on themselves. His lungs were burning, and he felt the world around him beginning to spin out of control. Patrick could feel great strength from Christkind's grip. He did whatever he could to harness Kris's force and use it to get himself upright again.

Kris looked into Patrick's glazed eyes. He knew from experience exactly what was going through the mind of his exhausted friend. He had been Santa for a very long time, but had not forgotten the many times where he felt the same reservations and doubts, as well as the temptation to quit.

Kris shouted his demand towards his partner. "Don't stop! It's downhill from here and then we get the wind at our backs! Come on Patrick! We can do this!"

Patrick regained his posture and looked at Kris. Kris reached out his fist and held it in the air. Patrick took a deep breath and acknowledged him by raising his fist and touching Kris's in return. Looking down the hill, Patrick could see the barn in the hazy distance, and began to make the trek downwards. John, down below, gave a sigh of relief that he had not killed his team and began to coach the men again, through his commanding shouts.

The men continued to push themselves. The earth's surface was uneven, covered in nature's debris and layered in thick snow. Patrick quickly had to work the core of his body and learn where to find his balance. He did not want to find himself face first; falling down the rough hillside, and embarrassing himself in front of the others.

As soon as they reached the bottom of the hill, John greeted them with a clap of his hands and shouted praises to them. But before the winded Patrick and Kris could come to a stop from the downward motion, John had turned and began to run forward, creating a new trail towards the barn, parallel to the ones they created moments ago. Although they had hoped to stop, if only for a few seconds, Patrick and Kris followed Mr. Dreiling and continued on. They knew that they would soon reach their home base and would be allowed to rest.

Like three men making an escape from prison, everyone put the rest of their strength into raising their feet above the snow, making large strides without tripping and collapsing, and risking being caught. Returning to the barn structure was like a reward after climbing the small mountain behind them. They continued moving forwards, listening to John Dreiling's instructions, and keeping vigilant of anything lying on the ground blocking their path back to the warmth that awaited them at home base.

All three men reached the barn doors, not stopping until they were able to reach out and touch the wooden hatch. As Patrick and Kris came to a stop, they each slumped forward and rested the weight of their bodies, by placing their hands on their knees to catch their breath. John gave his athletes just a moment, as he too managed to catch his breath. He then looked at the men and rewarded them with a more gentle voice. Still regaining his breath, he wanted to give his small team some encouragement.

Very winded, John attempted to speak to his team. "You both did well. I'm sorry I hit you so hard with such a large first step, but we only have three short weeks to get you as conditioned as possible. Neither one of us are as young as we use to be, but I for one am not ready to let you throw in the towel and get some replacement that has no-way near the spirit of Christmas that you two have. My purpose is to push you as hard as I can. My job is to make sure I push you till you drop. And when you get back up, I'm going to drop you again, and again, until you can't stand anymore."

As their lungs began to settle and their breathing returned to normal, Patrick and Kris stood upright and listened to what John was saying.

John continued. "Santa and I have been doing this for so long that sometimes we get complacent and try to cut corners. But last year, Kris nearly lost his life to the elements. I wouldn't have been able to live with myself if I would have had to approach Pinky and tell her that Santa was dead, knowing that we didn't put one hundred percent of ourselves into Christmas."

Christmas training had officially begun. Even though they were only forty-five minutes into their regimen, Patrick felt like he had just been through an entire week's worth of hell and was ready to crash onto a warm bed. John opened the barn doors and waited for Patrick and Kris as they made their way inside. He smiled with pride and then he closed up the building behind them.

CHAPTER SEVEN

Kris led Patrick to the small kitchen-like area and prepared a bottle of water for each of them to use throughout the morning. With a small toast, the two inhaled all their water and then immediately refilled them again to quench their thirst.

Patrick wanted to know more about his new companion. "So, how long have you been doing this, and how do you maintain it, year after year?"

Kris took another drink before answering Patrick's question. "I'd say a little more than three decades worth. Usually, the final couple months before Christmas are the hardest. For the rest of the year, it's just like going to the gym, and Mr. Dreiling's curriculum is much more casual and relaxing. It looks scary and it obviously feels scary, but in three weeks when we take flight, you'll be ready. I promise."

After a few moments to rehydrate, John called them back in to action. He wanted them to get started on weights before they cooled down to the point where it would be impossible to get their motivation back. With a clap of Mr. Dreiling's hands, the men made their way.

Back in the heart of the room, John awaited the men with an old fashioned weight lifting bench, surrounded by other steel weights and machines of various sorts and sizes. As Kris took his place on the first bench, John instructed Patrick to take his place on a leg press next to Kris, and then gave his team the instructions they would need for the next forty-five minutes.

John spoke clearly to Patrick and Kris. "The machine you are on is your beginning and ending location. Look around you. Notice that there are several stations. Once I tell you that you are done with your first spot, you will have 30 seconds to make it to your second station and be prepared for my signal. When working the bench press, I will be spotting you. At some stations, you will see additional accessories for your safety. Do not overlook this! If you see a belt, I expect you to put it on. I want you to build your strength but I want safety to be first in our minds. If I see that you are not being smart, I will stop you immediately. Do you understand?"

Patrick understood John's instructions and gave him a nod. He chuckled as he thought to himself. He never associated cross fit training as a vital part of the Christmas experience.

John nodded his head and gave the command. "Okay, let's get to it!"

And with Mr. Dreiling's signal, the clock began counting as Patrick and Kris began putting all their might into the machines they occupied. Patrick lay on his back, crawling under the leg press machine. With a modest two hundred pounds at his feet, Patrick pushed up with as much force as he could give, until his legs were fully extended. He then lowered the weights until they were back at the resting positions and immediately pushed the weight upwards again. Up and down in repetition, Patrick pushed and pushed, working every muscle in his legs until john gave the command to stop and move to the next weight station.

Getting up as quickly as he could, Patrick moved to the arm curling station and picked up two twenty pound dumbbells as he waited for Dreiling's command. Adrenalin was beginning to pump through Patrick's system. He was ready.

John looked at his men to see that they were both in place and then looked down to his watch. He focused on the second hand as it made its way to the top of the minute. Just as soon as the hand struck twelve, John gave the instruction and the men went right back to work.   John   shouted loudly. "GO!"

For forty-five minutes, Patrick was put through the gauntlet, working every muscle in his body. Muscles he hadn't worked in decades and had completely forgotten even existed. From station to station, Patrick pushed and pulled, up and down, in and out; giving everything he had in him for several moments at a time, and then rewarding himself with thirty seconds of rest before the next grueling test.

As the moments passed and as the men became familiar with the different stations, they began to help motivate each other with words of encouragement, as well as, physical gestures, such as patting and clapping. The three men were becoming a team, which is what it was going to take to become a successful unit.

Once every weight station had been completed, the men were given another water break. Patrick sat on a nearby bench and grabbed his bottle, drinking what was left within the vessel. He was covered in sweat. This morning had been long and grueling, and every muscle in his body was throbbing. As he tried to drink his water, he rested his head on the wall, trying to catch some sort of nap. Mr. Dreiling watched the men as they tried to mend their aches and pains by being as still as possible. John knew that he had succeeded in orientating his team. He called them over to him so that he could give them a word before releasing them for lunch.

As the men made their way to Mr. Dreiling, they spotted food waiting for them, over by the kitchenette area. While the men were working out for the morning, John had the ranch chef and his crew, prepare a high protein lunch for Patrick and Kris. Patrick was so happy to see the plate of food sitting there, as it meant that he was going to be given ample time to rest up before the afternoon sessions.

As soon as the men spotted the crew placing the food onto the table, Patrick and Kris gave a holler in celebration. John tossed the men a fresh steaming wet hand cloth as well as a warm towel so that they could clean up a bit before eating. As the men cleared away the sweat from their hands and faces, the chef and his crew finished serving the table for them.

John placed his hands on the men's shoulders. "Smells delicious, doesn't it?"

All three men found their mouths watering from the aroma of the freshly prepared meal. They were all ready for a break and eager to get down to lunch.

Before releasing them, John wanted to get in one last word. "In the early morning, David left his flock and set out for the Valley of Elah where his brothers were assembled with an army of Israelites. The soldiers stood terrified as they were about to take battle against the Philistines and their champion, Goliath. A giant among all men, Goliath came forward and took a stand against the Israelites putting terror into them, forcing the soldiers to flee. But God had another plan. He chose David, the small shepherd boy, over all of the Israelite soldiers, to go up against the giant. He spoke to David and told him of his purpose. David listened and put his faith into God's command. The next morning, David, armed with only a sling, reached down and grabbed five smooth stones for his artillery. As Goliath stood at the front line taunting the Israelites, David took his stand and slung a stone at the giant, striking him in the head and killing him, confirming victory over the Philistines."

John closed by saying, "In the natural, everyone thought that David would have been killed by Goliath, but David gave his strength to God instead of focusing on his abilities in the natural world. Because of this, God favored David and gave him the tools to defeat the giant and bring peace back to the Israelites. As for us, we will continue to focus on God for our strength and through him, this Christmas, we too, will be victorious."

John was not one to pray, but he could tell stories in a manner that came across as prayer. After his words of strength, John wished Patrick and Kris a Merry Christmas and the men dug in for supper.

For several minutes, the men sat and ate, enjoying the company and creating their camaraderie together. Focusing on the moment and taking their minds off of the aches and pains that continued to dwell within each of them. Patrick simply enjoyed the time they were allotted. He knew that this break was soon to pass and the afternoon would bring more torment, soon enough.

Once the meal was finished, and their bellies were full, restoring the team's energy, John stood from the table and gave the signal. With a command, the three men returned to their places in the center of the barn room, and they went back to focusing on training.

For the rest of the afternoon, Patrick endured the most physical experience of his life. With each workout, he was reminded of his youth and the types of warm-ups that they would perform during gym class throughout the year. The afternoon session began with stretches, forcing each muscle to reach out and extend in a way Patrick had not asked of them for a very long time. Once the calisthenics were completed, Patrick was tossed a jumping rope, where he began leaping in place, concentrating on his footing with each pass of the rope so than he would not find himself tripped up. He skipped and jumped and with every hopping movement, he could feel his ankles crying out to his calf muscles who were begging the knees and thighs to put more effort into each short bursting launch.

As Patrick and Kris continued their pace, John walked over and approached a nearby stereo. He pulled a vinyl record from its sleeve and placed the disc onto the circular platform. Then with a flip of a switch, Mr. Dreiling applied power to the record machine, giving the vinyl disc motion. He then placed the needle in its proper position and music began to echo throughout the barn gym.

The sounds of the orchestra took Patrick's mind off of the task at hand, allowing a warming joy to flow through his veins and creating a heightened strength for his body.

At Mr. Dreiling's command, the jump rope marathon was complete. Patrick threw down his rope in victory before quickly making his way to the next position. Along with Kris, the two waited for their instructor's next directions.

John showed the men what lay ahead. He pointed to several painted lines that lay in front of their path. Pointing back and forth, Patrick knew what he had to do. With the sound of John's familiar signal, both Patrick and Kris shot from their place and sprinted forward to the other side of the gym. They reached down to touch the marker and then turned and darted back to their home base. Back and forth, Patrick raced from line to line, bending down to touch the floor at every designated point. Once completed, John gave Patrick and Kris just a couple seconds to catch their breath before starting them on the next task. After each exercise, there was another one, and then another, and another. John wanted to work them hard and in short intervals, attempting to give an even workout to every joint and every muscle in their bodies.

Once the cardio exercises were checked off the list, John brought the men to the scaling wall and gave a thorough explanation to the basics of climbing. From there each man took their turn on the wall where they learned to use their upper and lower muscles in concert, learning to push and pull themselves upward while keeping their stability.

Kris was very familiar with technical climbing. He helped give instruction to Patrick as he slowly attempted his first turn on the steep wall, up to the loft above. Kris had used these techniques hundreds of times as he climbed around on each rooftop and made his way down the thousands of chimneys, leading to the living rooms below.

At the top of the wall, Patrick made his way to the loft where Kris stood, coaching and encouraging him. Kris helped him out of his harness and they tossed them down below to where John was waiting to catch.

John then waved up to both the men. "Okay guys. Let's go get something to drink!"

Mr. Dreiling was getting thirsty himself from all the shouting. He left the men in the loft and made his way to the kitchenette area.

Unsure why he had been left up there, Patrick looked at Kris for wisdom on how to get back down from the loft. Kris laughed and pointed downward to a large pile of hay below.

Kris chuckled. "Ever hear of a leap of faith?"

And with that, Kris darted out into the open air and plummeted down to the soft pile of straw, where he gently landed as if it were a billowy cloud. Kris stood to his feet and brushed himself off with a childlike giggle. He then looked upward to Patrick with a motion of his hand.

Patrick was not sure he had the courage for such a leap. He stood thinking about the endless possibilities of what could go wrong. He didn't want to end up dead, and gamble his return home to Katie.

However; Kris knew exactly what was racing through Patrick's mind. "You will endure this and you will see her again. You are here on a mission from God now, just like David. I don't think he would send you here, just to die in a dumb 'ole pile of hay! Trust and jump! Stop thinking about the natural and put your faith in him!"

Patrick agreed that he had been given this second chance at life for a reason. After contemplation he knew what he had to do and he hopped downward. Like a soaring baseball into a leather glove, Patrick was caught by the straw without any harm at all. Kris helped him to his feet and congratulated Patrick for taking his first of many leaps to come.

After the break, Mr. Dreiling left to attend the other stable attendants and look over the ranch for the afternoon. Kris took Patrick back to the toyshop where they would spend the rest of the day. He thought it would be good for Patrick to sit in one of their classrooms so that he could get a refresher course on Christmas history. Kris also wanted to educate Patrick through flight school and a few other classes to help him succeed this coming eve of Christmas.

Entering the class, Patrick found a box of notebooks and pencils and took one of each. He then made his way to the front of the room and took his seat. Except for a large Christmas tree in the corner of the lecture hall, the room where Patrick was going to study was not unlike that of any other classroom he had attended as a boy. Looking around the place there were posters about Christmas history on the wall, as well as atmospheric charts, and even lessons on space weather.

Mr. Christkind entered the room, accompanied by one of the elves. Kris and his helper sat at the desk for a moment and quickly flipped through a book, where Kris pointed out several items to cover. Kris then looked over to Patrick and smiled.

Kris introduced Patrick to his new teacher. "Patrick, please meet Ms. Joy Joyance. Joy is our top teacher and she will be spending the remainder of the afternoon with you. I've got to run but will leave you in her capable hands. I need to go check on an issue in Baking. Seems they have a dispute on whether the new funnel cake dispenser is working properly. I'm going to go have a bite and give my decision."

Kris left the room laughing, leaving Patrick in the care of Ms. Joyance. As Patrick and Ms. Joyance were making their introductions, the doors opened at the back of the lecture room and several students began making their way into the class, down the rows, and to their desks. As the students made their preparations, they murmured amongst themselves about the new human who was in the class with them. Patrick knew he was the white elephant in the room. But even though he felt a little out of place, he knew that eventually he would return to Ellinwood and would look back at this experience as the most important chapter in his life.

After taking their seats, Ms. Joyance asked the room to quiet down and come to attention. She then explained to them that they would be continuing their studies on the History of Christmas as well as the Theory of Workshop and Gifting. She then asked them to open their books to where they left off. Knowing that everyone in the classroom was looking at Patrick, she announced that they had a visitor who would be joining them. Introducing Patrick, she asked her class to be courteous to Mr. Wolf and to help her by assisting him during class. Patrick stood up and looked around the room at the students and with a smile he said "Hello." The students welcomed him and then everyone prepared to continue their studies. Making himself comfortable, he was ready to listen intently and learn as much as possible from Joy's lecture.

Ms. Joyance adjusted her glasses and looked around the classroom. "Okay everyone, who remembers where we left off from last time?"

A small young lady sitting next to Patrick raised her hand high into the air to catch the attention of her teacher. Ms. Joyance smiled and recognized her eager pupil.

The young student arose to her feet and answered her teacher. "You were about to cover the laws of low orbit flight travel and how it relates to the Earth's rotation."

Patrick's eyes grew wide and he looked over to his neighboring student in complete awe. A fear overcame him, and he worried that he may not be intelligent enough for a class that was covering the laws of low orbit travel.

Ms. Joyance saw the shocked look on Patrick's face and laughed to herself.

After a short pause, the student let Patrick off the hook. "Just kidding! You were about to explain to us how mass toy production was introduced to the North Pole."

With a sigh of relief, the classroom began to fill with laughter. Obviously, Patrick had just become the victim of a harmless classroom hazing. He looked over to the young student who was smiling back at him, along with the rest of the class. He then took his hand and wiped his brow. Patrick then reclined back into his seat and shook his head, like a good sport.

Ms. Joyance grinned as she lowered her head and looked over the top of her glasses towards the comedic students. "That's correct. We were about to discuss how Mr. Henry

Ford's invention of the sequential production of the car, influenced our toy making, here at the North Pole."

Patrick whipped out his pencil and began taking notes as Ms. Joyance began her afternoon lectures. Ms. Joyance was a brilliant instructor and made sure that she did not speak above the education level of Patrick and the other students. Patrick annotated everything that his teacher spoke. He was excited to learn how the Toyshop became an important part of Christmas History.

Between classes, the other pupils would approach Patrick to introduce themselves and learn more about him. The elves were extremely kind to their new guest, and Patrick learned quickly that elves were naturally good hosts, creating a culture of kindness throughout the community. Although this type of culture came naturally to the town of Ellinwood, when he was a young man, over the decades he saw this type of selflessness begin to fall further away from society, not only in his home town, but throughout the entire world.

Patrick enjoyed the classroom very much, and by the end of the afternoon, he was eager for the next day's lectures to come. He also looked forward to bringing his new Christmas knowledge back to Ellinwood and rebooting the excitement of the Christmas season back at home.

Following dinner back at the ranch, Patrick took a few moments to go into Kris and Pinky's solarium to watch the northern light shower illuminate the Arctic sky. Patrick had accepted this chapter in his life and was prepared to put all his effort into helping on Christmas Eve. Nonetheless, a part of him was still doubtful that he could bring success to Kris and the elves, and he worried that he would never see Katie again. He believed that Katie was continuing her vows to him by visiting him daily. It made Patrick feel guilty, knowing his family was under the impression that he was dying, when in reality, he was alive and well. He wished he could simply reach out to everyone at home and let them know he was just fine, but he knew the consequences would be more damaging than if he remained patient and just accepted his purpose for this Christmas Eve.

Pinky and Kris gathered in the family room, around the fire place, as they did most evenings. They discussed the day as they enjoyed the evening together. As they talked about the day's events and expressed their ideas about the preparation for Christmas, Pinky could not help but wonder what was bothering Patrick. Pinky was very in tune to the moods of those she loved. She was known as the mother of the North Pole, because of her sincere friendship with others. She watched Patrick for a while before she decided, that by allowing him to keep his worries to himself, she would be helping to bring failure to him.

Pinky leaned over and whispered to her husband. "Honey, go into our room and bring me that package I have sitting on the bed. I think now would be a good time."

Kris was not surprised at the perfect timing of his wife's request. Pinky loved gift giving, and one of her strongest ice breakers was through the giving of a present. Kris stood to his feet and kissed Pinky on the cheek. He then made his way to the bedroom to retrieve Patrick's surprise.

Pinky looked over at Patrick and asked him if he could help her attend the fire by adding a couple more logs to it, before retiring for the evening. He was more than eager to help his host. He made his way into the family room where Pinky thanked him for his help. Pinky was more than capable of adding wood on her own, but she wanted Patrick to start feeling at home in her house. As Patrick was adding the wood, Kris re-entered the room and took a seat next to his wife.

Once the fireplace was fueled and roaring again, Patrick remained with the Clauses upon their request to join them. Pinky again thanked Patrick for coming to the North Pole to help Kris this year. She told Patrick that their house was now his. She then asked him to please feel free to take advantage of all its amenities and to make himself at home.

Pinky then asked her guest to have a seat. "Patrick, I was thinking of you today, and about all the sacrifices you are making this year to help us, and I wanted to give you a gift."

With a wink, Pinky nodded to Kris as his cue to offer the package to their guest. Kris grabbed the gift-wrapped box and carried it over to Patrick.

Patrick smiled and his cheeks grew red. He took the package into his hands and sat it on his lap. He had not received a surprise present in a long time and was not exactly sure how to react.

As he accepted the package, he looked over to his friends and blushed. "Kris, did you know about this?"

Kris tried to act as if he knew nothing about it. "Absolutely not! I'm just as surprised as you are. Go ahead! Rip that present open so I can see what you got!"

Patrick pulled the brilliant red ribbon from around the box and then sank his fingernails into the wrapping paper and tore it off. He then delicately opened the box, exposing what was hidden within. Within the package was yet, another box. Patrick pulled the second package out and opened it to see what was inside. As soon as he looked upon the item that the Clauses had gifted him, Patrick became overwhelmed. He looked down in shock and then closed his eyes, in an attempt to hold off the tears of happiness that were beginning to make their way onto his cheeks. He then looked up to Pinky and Kris in wonderment.

Patrick spoke in shock: "I thought I had lost this forever."

Patrick held up his present to show his hosts what he was in possession of. Between his fingers he held an old metallic ring.

Patrick tried to get the words out without crying. "This was my father's ring. He gave it to me before he died. I used to wear it as part of my Santa uniform because, when I did, I felt that my dad was there living the experience with me. He was my inspiration to be Santa. As long as I wore this ring, I felt empowered and thought that I could never fail in my Santa responsibilities."

Patrick had lost the ring on Christmas Eve, several years ago. It was the first year that he could remember feeling that his purposeful role was no longer reaching others, and that his part of Santa was, somehow, invalid. Losing the ring put a doubt into Patrick that season. And for every year after that, he continued to lose more faith in his purpose and even himself.

The ring had been restored. The Clauses had the piece of jewelry recast and the gold that had been worn away was replaced. Patrick could see the designs throughout the ring just as they looked when he was a child. The brilliant red ruby had been polished and looked new again, except for a chip in the stone that was still there. Patrick had never seen the ring without the blemish. The ring had been restored but not to its original state. It was brought back to the day when Patrick first fell in love with his father's ring, many decades ago.

Kris explained to Patrick. "I ran across it last Christmas when you prayed for it to be found. Pinky had the brilliant idea to have the elves put some tender loving care into it, so we could return it to you this Christmas. But then you ended up here, so it just made sense to give it to you now."

Patrick was indeed very grateful for this gift. He thanked Pinky and Kris for bringing the ring back into his life and promised to never lose it again. Pinky freely wept with joy as Kris tried to hold back the contagious emotions.

Pinky impatiently shook her hands with anticipation. "Well? Put it on! I want to see you model it."

Patrick placed the ring back onto the finger that it once called home. It fit perfectly, and Patrick was happy to have it back in his possession. He held up his hand with pride and showed it off to the Clauses. Pinky took her camera and took a photo of the moment so she would never forget the look on Patrick's face. She truly believed that such jubilation should never be forgotten.

With the ice broken, Kris decided he wanted to know more about the years that led Patrick to lose faith in his self. Kris knew that if he was going to help restore Patrick's faith in life, that the ring alone would only be temporary. Patrick was brought to the North Pole because of his dying belief in Christmas and humanity. It was going to be Kris's responsibility to show Patrick that his Santa role was not in vain. He was going to have to make Patrick see life in a way he was too blind to see before his heart attack. This way, when he was returned home on Christmas Eve, Patrick's heart would be fully restored. When Patrick returned, he would be a new man, not only for himself, but for his family and his entire community.

As Patrick gazed up from his newly finished ring, Kris relaxed back into his seat and made himself more comfortable.

Kris then spoke to Patrick, "So Patrick, I have heard many wonderful things about your wife and your children. Pinky and I would love to get to know all about you. After all, whether you like it or not, you are now officially part of our family, and we only know a small portion of what makes you so special."

When Patrick heard Kris mention "family," he smiled. He knew that this time with the Clauses was short term but felt too, that they were just like family. Just like Kris was saying. Patrick wanted to know as much about everyone at the ranch as they wanted to know about him, so he agreed that this very moment was the perfect time to open up.

Patrick began to talk about his family, and as he reminisced, he began to smile. "My wife Katie, is my best friend in the whole world. We met at a very early age and quickly became friends. She was there for me for my broken arm and my tonsil surgery. She was at my side when my dog died. We went through everything together, so it only made sense that when it came to falling in love, that Katie was the one. We had two children. A boy and a girl, Jena and Patrick Junior, and together, we became the Wolf family. Katie has always taken care of the home, but she's not a house wife in the traditional sense. She reminds me of you, Pinky. She always gets out around town, getting involved in the church and the schools. She loves anything she can get her hands on, trying to help others. She's really my hero. She loves people, even those who don't want to be loved. I don't think I have that gift. I am more selfish and, sometimes, I just need a little push to get out around other people."

Patrick looked over to his hosts who were listening intently. "It's funny, I play Santa, and everyone loves me as Santa. For the entire month of December, I feel like a celebrity to everyone who sees me. That beard hid my shyness towards others and allowed me to be the magical being the kids wanted me to be. In time, it even allowed me to open up towards others and make many good friends. Katie knew from the very beginning, that I loved Christmas, just a little more than most. I loved the pageantry behind the months leading to Christmas Day. I felt the calling to be Santa, and Katie was probably the one that opened my mind to the calling. She went out and bought me a very nice Santa suit that I wore for my entire career, up until just last year."

Kris had seen Katie through his journeys. Through those very short moments, he knew about her kind heart. She also reminded him of Pinky. Patrick's marriage to Katie was another one of the reasons why he was selected to partake in this year's Christmas.

Kris wanted to offer a little hope to Patrick. "You are still very young and obviously, extremely fit. Why did you decide to hang up your Santa suit so early in life?"

Patrick's smile began to wander off to another place as he thought about it for a short moment. The decision he had made was not in haste. He had spent years in contemplation, but it wasn't until this very year that he finally felt content with his decision to retire.

Patrick scratched his head and answered Kris's question. "When I was a child, Christmas was so magical. I never wanted to lose that feeling. I never wanted anyone else to lose that either, so Katie told me that if I felt so strongly about keeping the Christmas traditions alive, that I was going to have to lead by example and be Santa. When she told me to be that leader, it was as if she had just turned on a light bulb in my head, so I did just that. I became Santa!"

Looking up to the ceiling, Patrick smiled in thought. "It was so awesome! I enjoyed showing up and seeing the excitement on the kids' faces as they saw me. They would stand in line, looking around each other hoping that the line would speed up. When they sat on my lap, they poured out their tiny little hearts and let me know what they desired. It was probably one of the few moments they were completely honest with anyone. They felt like they could tell me anything. And, that whatever they told me would be what would happen. It was amazing indeed."

Patrick looked over towards Kris with a grin and continued on. "You see, I got to see something as Santa that you did not. I got to see the smiles on their faces when they looked me in the eye. The expressions on their faces glowed with love and trust."

Kris nodded his head in agreement. As Santa, he was a traveler of the night and did not have the luxury to see those young smiles that Patrick encountered.

Patrick's eyes then began to drift towards the floor. "But over time, our little community began to change. The entire town's culture began to shift. New ideas and beliefs were introduced, and I felt as if people thought I was a negative influence to the young children. And, by portraying myself as Santa, I was beginning to come across as antichrist like to the community."

Emotions began building up inside Patrick. He placed his hands on either side of his head. "Once, I was told that by being Santa, I was betraying my Christian beliefs. After hearing that, I bought into the whole thing. I even started acting like a fictional character, removing my beard so that the children could see I was not a real Santa. I wouldn't allow them to create a belief in my character, because I did not want to offend their parents. That's when the kids seemed to stop looking at me as some sort of a deliverer of hope and more as a stranger. So I stopped. I gave in, and helped an entire community lose their love for Christmas. And by doing so, by not portraying Santa properly, I lost faith in my purpose, my role as a husband and father, and my role as a friend to everyone I knew." Patrick hung his head low and grew quiet.

Kris too, had also seen changes to how he was perceived, over the years, and shot back with encouragement. "But look around you! You're here at the North Pole! You have seen the workshop and have met the elves. You are sitting in the same room with Santa and Mrs. Claus, and you too will take part in the trip around the big-wide-world! How many other Santas can say they have been able to do that?"

Patrick stood to his feet and looked out the window into the night sky. He looked at the glow of the Christmas lights as it illuminated the countryside. "Yes, and I thank you both. But, like the saying goes, "seeing-is-believing," and I can't make everyone at home see just how real you really are."

Pinky got up and walked over to Patrick. She then placed her gentle hand on his shoulder and spoke softly. "I bet that's how God feels about all of us at times."

Kris too rose to his feet. "As I've told you, over the years my job has become increasingly more difficult. It has put a lot of stress on me and my wife. Katie asked me to bring on help. I need someone like you to help me save Christmas. We hope that you will understand just how important you are to us and will help make that trip with me."

Patrick thought about it for not even a moment and then smiled again.

Kris was eager to know what Patrick was thinking. "So what are you going to do then?"

Patrick's smile grew wider and wider.

Pinky giggled with anticipation. "Well?"

Patrick laughed and looked back towards the two. "I'm going to help you succeed at Christmas this year and go home a better husband, a better father, and a better friend to everyone I know. More importantly, I'll never exchange my beliefs for those the world would rather I follow, ever again."

Pinky smiled brightly and spoke loudly with excitement. "Amen! We are so happy to have you here this year."

Kris, too, shared his wife's feelings. "We are indeed, very grateful. Pinky, you should have seen this man at work today. If he keeps it up, he might put me out of business, and I may have to go live in Ellinwood, instead!"

Kris then stretched out his back and held out his arms as he let out a deep yawn. "We better get to bed. Tomorrow will be here soon enough and I, for one, am going to need every minute of sleep I can get."

The first day of training had been very demanding, and both Patrick and Kris were ready to find their soft warm beds, leaving the day behind them.

Mr. Christkind took his wife by the hand and escorted her into their quarters. Patrick admired their love very much.

Although it made him miss his Katie, Patrick was excited because he knew that soon, he would be making his journey home.

Patrick made his way to his room and climbed into the bed. Feeling the cold attempting to make its way under the sheets, Patrick wrapped himself tightly inside the warm blankets, fighting off the chill, and then fell deep into sleep.

CHAPTER EIGHT

With what only seemed like moments, Patrick awoke from the sound of clanging metal from the vintage alarm clock, echoing throughout his room. After slapping the tattler into silence, Patrick rubbed his eyes. Then he began the process of convincing himself to leave his warm bed so that he could get dressed.

Although Patrick had fallen asleep feeling quite comfortable and relaxed, when he awoke his body ached from head to toe. With every little movement, he felt his muscles scream at him, as if to tell him to just stay in bed. But before long, he finally left the comfort of his bunk and raced to see just how fast he could get his clothes on. Once dressed, he sat out from the house and made his way through the fresh snow that fell throughout the night.

Patrick opened the entry door to the barn, and immediately found a hot breakfast waiting on him. Without any questions, he sat at the table and began to consume his meal.

John Dreiling heard the stirring from the other room and peeked inside to see who was at the table. He came in to wish him a good morning, and the two exchanged their greetings. From outside, the door opened and Kris quickly entered. He then saw that he was the last to the party and chuckled as he joined the men for breakfast.

Not many words needed to be spoken. The men were tired and sore, and what was worse, they all knew that more aches and pains were waiting on them. After Patrick finished his breakfast, he began stretching his arms and legs, walking around the room, trying to get limber. Seeing the old record player across the room, he approached the stereo system and looked at the collection of vinyl on the shelf. Taking his finger, he ran it across the wide selection of music until he spied just the right motivation that he had been looking for. He had found rock music to his favorite Christmas songs. With a victorious nod, Patrick was ready.

The music began jumping from the stereo speakers, arcing through the air, and bouncing off the barn walls. Patrick looked over to his team to see what they thought of his taste in music. John gave Patrick the thumbs up motion, in approval to his selection. He then stood up and slapped his hands and announced the beginning of the day.

The morning twilight was all the men needed to see the path before them. Patrick and Kris ran throughout the entire ranch, gaining strength through the deep snow areas, and picking up speed in the shallow spots. As they ran, from out of nowhere, the reindeer began to appear around them, running with them. John too, joined the group of athletes, standing on a snowboard type sled, pulled by Rudolf. Together, the twelve souls ran and ran, like a well-orchestrated regimen. Patrick could not help but smile at the view of all of them working together.

As they passed over the hill, the workshop came into view. The team continued forward, towards the building, still a couple miles away. But as they approached, a few of the elves spotted the team heading their direction. They quickly spread the word around the shop and the elves began leaving their posts in order to see the rare sight. Soon, the thousands of elves stood watching and cheering, so that the men and the deer would hear them.

Patrick could hear the roaring army of elves supporting them as they approached the shop. Looking over to Kris, he could see the smile on his face, beaming with great pride, as the entire village expressed their support. Patrick raised his arms in victory for the little on-lookers sake. The already loud cheering became quite deafening in response to the runners feeding the team's egos and giving them the encouragement they needed to keep pushing forward.

The group continued their morning run, passing the workshop, and then down into the nearby valley where finally they disappeared in the trees.

Although the collaborated moment was brief, it had been an inspiring run for everyone. Back at the barn, Patrick, Kris, and John broke from the deer and went inside for some weight training. The reindeer proceeded forward to a nearby field, where they were going to continue their own instructions. The men, still excited from the toyshop experience went directly to their first weight lifting stations, where John immediately shouted out his commands and started timing their workouts.

With each clap of Dreiling's hands Patrick moved from station to station. The display of appreciation that the elves had given him had increased his desire to give his best effort on the weight machines. The elves at the workshop also shared the same appreciation from watching the men and the deer make an appearance that morning. The sense of adrenaline had contagiously spread throughout the entire workshop. And although the elves were always proficient at their jobs, today there was a unique excitement in the air. The unusually high spirits could be felt by everyone that entered the building that day.

Talk was spreading through the toyshop of the iconic moment. As Pinky entered the building, she immediately noticed more music and singing from the elves than normal. Unable to ignore the excitement in the atmosphere, she too began to smile and sing Christmas songs under her breath, as she made her way throughout the shop.

Throughout the day, Patrick pushed himself as hard as he could. As he flipped the giant tractor tires, he thought of Katie. As he climbed the walls, he thought about how proud Patrick Junior would be of him. And, when he sat in class, he thought about his daughter, Jena, as she was a school teacher back at home. Patrick kept his mind focused on his family. He was going to return home a brand new man and wanted nothing more but to enjoy every coming moment with them. He promised himself that this was going to be the best Christmas he had ever known.

The entire first week of training brought demands upon Patrick that he was not prepared for. The physical workouts were familiar to him. From his high school years, up to the present day, Patrick had always tried to maintain a good physical condition. However, he had not pushed his bodily limits to these extremes in nearly thirty years. Day in and day out, he allowed himself to endure the beatings, not only from John Dreiling's daily regimens, but from the arctic environments that brought forth impossible extremes, famously known to kill any life form in its path. On top of the physical drawbacks of being at the North Pole, Patrick had to deal with his own personal demons that were working overtime, pushing him to quit, assuring defeat to himself, and bringing failure to all of Christmas.

Throughout the North Pole, everyone was beginning to learn about Patrick's story, as well as his extraordinary sacrifices. Many of the elves were so inspired by his graciousness, that they began to send him hand written letters thanking him for coming to the North Pole and helping Mr. Christkind with this year's journey. Everyone's minds were on Kris's health this year. Although he was perfectly capable to travel solo, the last trip was full of many close calls and many scares, which had taken a toll on his body. Kris was still in recovery from last Christmas Eve, so when they learned of Patrick's arrival, he instantly became the focus of the city and their good luck charm.

At the end of each day, Patrick's body felt broken and his mental state, exhausted; but as the evenings passed, Pinky would make sure to deliver the letters to him to help raise his spirits. If he was too weak to read them, Pinky would sit down and read them aloud to him. Pinky wanted nothing more than for Patrick to find sanctuary at the North Pole, and with each letter of encouragement Patrick was fueled with the strength to continue. Nonetheless, Satan has a way to take all acts of kindness and silently whisper into the ears of the broken, inseminating the spirit of apprehension to work through their souls. Patrick received each and every letter from the elves and heard their kind-loving words. Those letters produced the energy that he needed to wake up each day and push on with an assault of vigor. But deep inside his thoughts, he was not at rest with his personal achievements. Because of his unbelief, a small seed of doubt lay quietly within him, patiently preparing to sprout.

God had given everyone freewill, so seeing himself as nothing else but victorious could only be done so by Patrick himself. Although he was the recipient of many supernatural blessings, Patrick's mind still processed the world in a natural way. Despite the fact that he had been brought to the North Pole through Godly forces, he struggled to understand that those same forces would guide himself through the days and bring victory to his mission.

Patrick felt his personal fears dwelling deep within himself but he also knew that there was not one individual at the North Pole who did not believe in his purpose there. Patrick began posting the letters on the walls of his room and on the walls of the barn. This way, if he ever found himself in a moment of doubt, he would only be a few short steps away from those inspirations.

Throughout the days, John Dreiling and Kris watched Patrick as he read the letters during their moments of rest. They saw the renewed determination inside him, through every card and letter. They even began to read the letters as well, and quickly, they understood how the elves were fueling his drive. Before long, all three men had incorporated those literary charms as a routine part of their long hours of training. Even though the Christmas Eve journey was vital to everyone at the North Pole, training for Christmas had a way of breaking a person's spirit. Those letters brought new forms of energy to all of them. Kris was proud of his elves for taking time out of their toy making deadlines and writing those letters. As their master, it overwhelmed him with happiness to see his North Pole family go out of their way, over and beyond what they had been employed to do, and offer such kindness to their visitor and new friend.

Each day, Patrick would leave the ranch and go to the workshop for classroom time and to experience the elves at work. With each of those passing days, he began to get to know his teachers and the toy-makers, just as he had been accustomed to do back at home. Patrick found that the folks at the North Pole were not unlike those down below. They were all individually unique in their own special ways. They all had different strengths and weaknesses, and their hopes and fears about life were no different than anyone he had ever known. Patrick was making new friends by the day. Throughout his entire life, Patrick had always joked and made fun of the ones he felt close to. It was his unconventional way of expressing endearment towards the ones he loved the most. Before long, his friendly essence spread throughout the workshop and Pinky could see how he was positively affecting the elves' performance.

An overall aura of unity spread like wildfire throughout the workshop, unlike ever before. A broken spirit at the North Pole was just as heart breaking as a death was to the rest of the world. Just like Patrick, over the past few years, Kris had begun to lose hope in his ability to be Santa. His diminished confidence could be felt by the elves even more than Kris could feel it within himself. But from the day that Patrick arrived, it was obvious to the elves that a renewed hope had been brought to this year's Christmas.

Back at the ranch, Christmas music filled the barn's gymnasium. John Dreiling loved good music. He felt that through music, a person could find the added strength needed to get through anything the forces of nature could throw at them. So for John, he made sure that music was present each day, to help keep Patrick and Kris's minds off the punishment he was demanding of them. A single week had passed since the beginning of their workouts, and John felt very confident in the progression of both his men. He only had two more weeks to get them ready for Christmas Eve. He was going to have to push them even harder to keep their drive up and to combat any possible loss of motivation.

At the end of the day, John Dreiling gathered his men. He wanted to be sure to give them a few words of inspiration before releasing them. He praised them for their hard work and told them that their performance had exceeded any of his original expectations. Not wanting to let their drive slow down, he told them that he was going to add something new to their regimen. Taking his hand, he held it up and pointed to the center of the barn where the only piece of untouched equipment remained.

In the very heart of the gym stood a full size octagonal shaped cage, where he would introduce Patrick and Kris to the world of hand-to-hand combat. In the recent past, the self-defense training had been mostly a basic form of education. However, over the seasons, Kris had experienced an increasing need to protect himself. Dreiling decided that this year he would put more focus on defending any of those unexpected threats.

John opened the doors to the cage and entered inside. Patrick and Kris followed behind him. Patrick had never been inside a fighting octagon before. He had watched many fights with his son through the television, so he was familiar with what happened in these cages. He imagined the fighters as they fought like gladiators in the chain-linked rings, and began to wonder what lay in wait for him. Kris, also, was no stranger to the fights that had occurred inside these steel enclosures. He was excited that John had built it for them. A growing concern for Kris was aimed directly at the fact that people around the world were getting increasingly more violent and that sooner or later, he would find himself in a situation that he would not be able to handle.

John Dreiling met the men in the middle of the ring. "Gentlemen, this is it! Starting tomorrow, we are going to add several forms of fighting disciplines to our day."

Patrick was a naturally stout person and was blessed with the gift of strength. The children of his youth did not have the technologies of the modern world, so the expectations of a child were greater than those of today's society. Back in his day, hard work and hard play helped Patrick to condition his body to be physically strong. Nevertheless, although Patrick had no issues striking things with great force, he had not hit another human being since he studied boxing in high school gym.

Patrick knew that in order to protect himself, sooner or later, he was going to have to come to terms about striking his partner. However, the thought of harming another person was simply not in his nature.

Kris too had mixed thoughts running through his head. Being Santa Claus was never intended to be violent. Carrying on the mission of Saint Nicholas was meant to be about spreading God's love around the world, and he had always hoped that the same love would be returned to him. As he listened to John, he tried to think of a good reason why practicing hand-to-hand combat was not essential to the Christmas spirit, but the more thought he put into it, the more he came to accept the fact that if he did not learn to protect himself, he would put the entire Christmas Eve mission in great peril.

As always, Kris managed to find some humor in the depths of their new Octagon, and with John Dreiling, whom he held close to his heart, Kris looked at his friend and chuckled. "And, are you an expert in mixed martial arts now?"

Patrick, unsure how defensive training was conducted in prior Christmases, looked at Kris and then over to John for a response.

John laughed, and then turned and struck one of the punching dummies which stood in the ring, thrusting it into the metal mesh behind it. Patrick and Kris both stood in awe of the strength that Mr. Dreiling had just displayed for them.

John drew back his fist and looked over to the men. "Go finish your day, and then be sure to hit the beds early. Tomorrow, we'll begin."

As Patrick and Kris made their way to the house, a feeling of disorientation began to come across Patrick. Patrick was never one to allow himself to show others that he was in pain, but the feeling came on rapidly, and Patrick was not sure what was going on. He stopped walking and bent forward, bringing his hands out to his side for balance.

Kris watched Patrick intently, preparing himself to catch his friend at the first sign of collapsing. Kris watched closely and studied his every move.

After a short moment, Patrick returned to his upright position and looked over to Kris in confusion.

Kris spoke to Patrick with great concern. "Are you alright?"

Patrick was not sure what had just happened. He pressed his hand around his internal organs, feeling for something that might be out of place, or for some sort of breakage. He had felt a great uneasiness come over his body, but his physical self, seemed quite normal.

Perplexed, Patrick responded with confusion. "I don't know. I feel alright. I don't know what that was."

Patrick continued to check his body for anything out of the ordinary, but could find nothing alarming. "I saw my wife just now. She was crying."

After hearing what Patrick told him, Kris had an idea of what he had just experienced. Patrick's body was just fine; however, his old vessel was showing signs of fatigue.

The two continued to make the passage back to the ranch house. As they walked, Patrick brushed himself off as if what he experienced was simply a passing feeling, but for Kris, he could not help but to think his world back at home attempting to communicate with him in some way.

That evening at the toyshop, Patrick was sitting in class with Ms. Joyance and the other students. They were discussing Christmas literary history. Ms. Joyance was covering the story of the Christmas Carol and how each of the ghosts, and their messages to Ebenezer Scrooge, were still relevant in today's society.

As Patrick sat and listened. His thoughts of home and Christmas Past began to flood his mind. He was reminded of the moments in his life when times were not so kind to him. With each of those experiences he thought about how his life was changed for the better and yet on some occasions, for the worst. Patrick, along with everyone that had ever lived upon the earth, had been sculpted through every involvement in his life. And, just like the others, the way he perceived the experiences led to how his life progressed.

He thought of his family and friends back in Ellinwood. He especially thought about the many events that happened throughout his life, and how his responses to those events molded him as a person. He had never claimed to be the perfect Santa Claus, but he was beginning to understand that every decision he made, every expression shown, and every word spoken towards his friends and family, spoke either life or death to them. That meant that his time as Santa had the power to affect the Christmas Spirit in all the children who believed in him.

Patrick did not want to be the tool that others used to diminish the magic of Christmas in the little children. As he was in thought, a vision of revelation came to him. Images of children from all over the world were waking up on Christmas morning full of pure joy. Patrick wanted nothing more than to create that joy in others. He decided that after returning home, he was no longer going to let the world dictate how he presented Santa towards the kids. He made a promise to himself that he was going to promote the true Christmas Spirit to everyone he was to meet. And, that he would teach them that Santa was not a pagan image, attempting to overshadow the birth of Jesus, but an iconic Christmas figure, selected by God, to deliver his love to others.

As usual, Patrick sat and absorbed every word spoken by Ms. Joyance. While she continued with her lecture, Kris stood outside of the classroom and watched through a little window in the door, not wanting to be seen as a distraction to the students. He enjoyed listening to the words of Ms. Joyance. She had a way of communicating with people and bringing out the best in everyone who heard her speak. Kris was enjoying what was being taught during Ms. Joyance's lecture. He could not help but to notice how Patrick was intently listening in her class. Never did Kris hold any reservations about bringing Patrick to the North Pole, and the sight of Mr. Wolf's eagerness in the classroom only validated Kris's decision. He thought about his role towards Patrick as his mentor. It was Kris's obligation to teach Patrick about Christmas so that he could go home a new man, and as he watched on, he began to worry about possibly failing his new friend.

Passing by, Pinky found Kris standing and watching the class through the window. It was not usual in her husband to just stop what he was doing, when so many toys were still in need to be built before Christmas Eve. For him to be so motionless, she knew that something was on his mind. Something he could not shake so easily. Pinky loved her husband very much and had always allowed him to portray his heroic persona to the others. However, she also knew he was just human, and from time to time, needed to receive the help of others. She walked up to Kris and placed her hand on his shoulder, gently, as not to frighten him from his deep thoughts.

Her familiar warm touch was most welcomed by her husband. He turned to her and greeted her with a gentle smile. He then took her by the hand and told her what was on his mind. "Patrick had an aura come over him this afternoon. I believe it was from his body, back at home. I think his body is starting to pass, and just after I made him that promise to bring him home."

Pinky's heart was always full of comfort towards others. She thought about what Kris had said but did not seem as concerned for Patrick as her spouse did. "Are you afraid for him? Do you honestly think his body is going to pass before Patrick can return home?"

Kris didn't answer. He didn't really know what to think.

Pinky kissed her husband on the cheek and laid her head on his shoulder. "You know better than that my love. You are not in charge of this, God is. You did not bring Mr. Wolf to us,

God did. Why would Patrick be given a second chance at life, just to find himself stuck here? I believe this is God's way of using Patrick's heart attack to become a testimony to others. I also believe that part of his testimony will be to generate new life into you, just as God had intended. I may not know exactly what is to happen to him, any more than I know what is to happen to me. Let me assure you that everything you are doing for him, he is doing the same for you as well. When this is all said and done, Patrick is going to succeed in his Godly purpose. And as for you, you will be the path that God used to accomplish that for him."

Pinky then took Kris and turned him away from the small window until he was facing her. She then smiled at him with confidence to show her spouse that she believed in him. "We've been given free will to accept our missions in life. If we allow ourselves to think only about the negative things that could happen, inevitably, we're just opening ourselves up for failure. That is not the Santa I know. Don't allow yourself to see Patrick's death. The only thing you need to do is help him get back home and allow him to work the magic that God has sent him here to do. And believe me. If this is truly God's purpose for Patrick, there is nothing you can do to make him change his mind. All you have to do is be the caring Santa I know you to be and help him the best you can. That's all. It's as easy as that."

Kris always appreciated the way Pinky brought perspective to any situation. She was right. If Patrick was here under supernatural circumstances, there was no reason to doubt that God would not see them through to the end. These same thoughts seemed to be working through both Patrick and Kris this year. For Pinky, it was obvious that they were brought together, not only to find their meaning in life but to save each other from their own personal demons.

Pinky kissed Kris on the lips and smiled again. She then placed her hand on her husband's cheek and pinched him lightly. "Don't let anything but goodness pass through you. You are my husband, but most importantly, you are our Santa. I believe in you. We all believe in you. Except nothing less than success and put the will of God before your fears. I promise you, if you do only that, God's purpose for you and Patrick will come to pass this year."

Kris smiled with enlightenment and thanked his wife. Around the North Pole, Kris may have been the big man on campus, but for him, Pinky was his true hero.

CHAPTER NINE

The next day, was the first day of the remaining two weeks until Christmas. With Kris at terms with helping Patrick learn to believe in himself again, and Patrick ready to help Kris succeed with his Christmas mission, the two sat out to the barn to train.

Inside the steel octagonal cage, the men stood in wait for Mr. Dreiling. Both were ready to take on this day and give whatever it would take to be the best crew that had ever flown on Christmas Eve. John entered the room carrying a large bag over his shoulder. Patrick and Kris watched him as he started the music and then approached the octagon. As he entered the cage, he threw the duffle towards the men, into the center of the ring. Kneeling down over the case, he unzipped the bag and reached inside. Looking up at Patrick and Kris, he tossed each of them a pair of grappling gloves.

With that, John wasted no time in beginning his instructions on how to throw punches and launch kicks. His intent was for the men to learn to strike their opponents with great force, but without hurting themselves in the process. Once confident that they were ready, Mr. Dreiling began to throw various combative moves at the men to see how well they could defend themselves. Dreiling only had two weeks left. In order to keep from wasting any of their remaining time together, he needed to know their skill levels and move forward from there.

Throughout the morning, Dreiling showed his students the various techniques of fighting hand to hand. Through the use of the punching dummy he pointed out where the most sensitive pressure points on the human body were located. There was still much to teach the men about protecting themselves, and Mr. Dreiling was going to make sure that when they were done they possessed the skills required to survive this year's journey. Patrick learned quickly from the techniques that Dreiling had shown him. Before the end of the morning, both he and Kris had learned the basic skills that they were going to continue to expand on for the remainder of their training. Although there was not enough time to mold them into professional MMA fighters, Patrick was more confident than ever that he would walk away from this, better prepared to defend himself.

That afternoon as Patrick and Kris entered the Workshop, they were greeted by the lead flight communications dispatcher, Francis. He wanted to bring attention to a few items that were developing in the lower countries, which could potentially affect their Christmas Eve journey. They followed him into a dark room full of digital monitors and blinking lights. Inside, the communications team was continually vigilant over the world's current affairs.

Francis brought up a map of the world and began to show his pilots various weather satellite images, along with long tracking forecasting models. He explained to Patrick and Kris how each of the models were all beginning to affect each other individually. Then he showed them how all the weather patterns would eventually collide on Christmas Eve. Polar weather fronts were currently making their way from the Alaskan regions, down toward the United States. According to Francis, the Great Lakes region, with a focus over the city of Chicago, was going to bring a violent polar storm to the upper north eastern states. And if the forecasts were correct, the storm would make navigation very dangerous to the crew and their team of reindeer. Francis explained to them the possibilities of severe icing on the sleigh and how it could affect the safety of the flight.

On top of the oncoming winter storm over the United States, Francis wanted to revisit a news story that they had been following for years. Although the news was nothing new to the communications team and to Kris, it was important not to forget its existence as it was very dangerous information. Francis brought up a news broadcast for them to watch.

Down south in the country of Afghanistan, a disturbance in Kabul had once again come to light and soldiers from around the world continued to gather in war. War was not new to everyone but it would affect the trip. Patrick had not thought about Christmas Eve in the Middle-East before. He watched intently with concern. Although this news worried Mr. Christkind very much, Kris looked at Patrick and winked at him.

This type of news was old hat to Kris, but like a good leader, he tried his best to put Patrick's fears aside. "Don't worry about a thing, my friend. This fight is older than you or I. We'll be okay as long as they can keep their cool."

As the news anchor spoke about the dangerous happenings in Kabul, Kris turned with Patrick and the two left the room to continue with their training.

Over the next two weeks Patrick worked harder than ever, with the demands of training for the big trip. With the winter storm and the news of Kabul on his mind, he took every moment very seriously. Although the news he had watched were items of concern, Patrick did not want to forget that his purpose was to help Kris on his trip. Even though Kabul and Chicago were never far from his mind, Patrick made the decision to focus on Christmas. He needed to get home to Katie, who was patiently waiting on him.

Each morning, Patrick conditioned himself to be ready for the day. He always woke very eager, as if it were the last day of school before Christmas morning. He found an excitement in jumping out of bed, with anticipation of what the new day would hold for him. Whether their morning was full of cardio or weight training, Patrick found a passion for each of the day's surprises. In the afternoons, the men underwent vigorous combat education, as well as flight training with a sleigh and reindeer. And during the evenings, Patrick focused on his class room training with Ms. Joy Joyance, along with learning how to make toys with the elves. And furthermore, he became extremely knowledgeable at the procedures of entering a home and delivering presents to the children without disturbing the household. With each passing evening, Patrick took time out to say a prayer for Katie and his family. Keeping God close to his heart, Patrick effortlessly fell asleep in excitement for the next mornings to come.

As everyone at the North Pole worked together to be ready for Christmas Eve, the world below continued with their everyday happenings. Katie had made the conscious decision that Patrick would want her to decorate the house in her traditional way. She brought out every Santa figurine in her mighty collection and spread them throughout the house. Her Santa collection was famous to the town of Ellinwood, and as for her grandchildren they were all magical in their own unique ways. Patrick Jr. and Jena packed for their trip to Nana Katie's house in order to be with her this Christmas. Even though Patrick's body lay brain dead in the hospital, his family prayed for him each day, in hopes that he would return to them. The doctors gave little hope of him waking up before Christmas day, but that didn't stop his family from deciding that they would be together.

Before Patrick's attack, the town of Ellinwood had put up their city Christmas decorations. Lining the major streets with large lit ornaments, they had prepared the entire down town to look like a Christmas wonderland. And while he was away, each of the schools had put on their holiday pageants for their parents and the town folk. This year, the high school decided to pay tribute to their local celebrity, Mr. Patrick Wolf, and support Katie through their love and appreciation for them. With the big day approaching, the children finished writing their letters to Old Saint Nick and put them in the mail, in hopes that they were not too late to tell Santa what they wanted for Christmas. Through Patrick's heart attack, the entire town of Ellinwood had found their holiday Spirit like never before.

The entire world had prepared for Christmas Day. For some, they had visions of waking up and sharing the big day with their families. For others, they had planned traditions of their own. While for even others, people stayed safely in their homes to avoid the turmoil's around them. Not one family would celebrate Christmas morning the same way. Nevertheless, even though they did not all experience the holiday with the same traditions or beliefs, they all recognized the day and respected its importance.

December 23rd had arrived at the North Pole. Patrick and Kris were a little over twenty-four hours from beginning their mission. Everyone around the entire earth had prepared for Christmas day, and very few items on their check lists were yet to be completed. As for the citizens at the North Pole, the elves worked overtime to finish their toy orders and have them wrapped for the trip. Patrick and Kris spent one final morning with Mr. John Dreiling. John had worked his men beyond their limits and prepared them, both mentally and physically, for their trip. The elves were nearly complete with their work for the year, making sure all the preparations for Santa and Patrick were ready for Christmas Eve.

Once the men were done with their final workout, the three made their way to the stables to meet with the caribou. The reindeer had trained hard for their journey, just like Patrick and Kris. Kris asked the men to join him at the stables to see the deer. He wanted to have one last moment with his team of stags, as he knew there would be very little time for words after today.

The reindeer were already prepared for Kris's annual visit, always held on the morning before Christmas Eve. They took their places and stood at attention upon hearing that their Santa was approaching. The deer were ready. They looked like mighty soldiers prepared for battle. And as the men came into the stables, right behind them, animals throughout the ranch filed in to be witness of Santa's iconic talk.

Knowledge of his entrance into the barn had also spread throughout the entire workshop. Kris's annual visit with the reindeer had become a historic tradition, and everyone in the North Pole looked forward to it each year. A microphone had been installed so that his speech could be enjoyed by everyone. The elves stopped what they were doing, just for a moment, so they could hear their Santa speak. Pinky took a seat, with coffee in her hand, and sat to watch the sun, just beyond the horizon and just behind the ranch. She had waited for this moment all year. She loved to listen to her husband's voice.

As Patrick and John stood with the deer, Kris took his place as Santa, in front of them. It was common knowledge throughout the world that Santa had the gift of speaking to animals. With his hands behind his back he walked in front of his crew and inspected each one of them with great honor. Kris could not find a single flaw amongst them. Even if he would have found something out of place, he held their character well above their appearance.

Making his way back to the center of the room, Kris looked down at the ground and smiled, as he thought about the many trips they had completed together throughout the years. Then after a short moment, he raised his head and looked his mighty caribou in the eyes. He then looked around to the rest of the animals who were there to hear him give his annual motto. The North Pole was guided on the principles of love for one another. The animals were not excluded from those same doctrines, and seeing such respect for all the critters, made Kris's heart overflow with joy. Patrick watched Kris and could see the proudness welling up inside him. He was stupefied as he had never seen a congregation like this ever before.

Kris smiled brightly at his team, and then around to everyone within the stable. "Merry Christmas, everyone!"

In their own given languages, the animals responded to Kris's welcoming words. For the rest, listening back at the toyshop, everyone shouted a Merry Christmas to their Master of Ceremonies. Patrick gazed around the room to witness the animals as they responded to Kris.

After his pause, Kris cleared his throat and then spoke. "Well, another Christmas is upon us. In the morning, we will take flight and do what very few living creatures ever get to do. Tomorrow, we get to go zooming around the big-wide-world."

"In just twenty-four hours, children across the globe will begin climbing into their little beds and praying to God one final time, petitioning him for whatever it is that they desire for Christmas. Each one of them has tried their hardest to be on their best behavior, in hopes for what is to come on Christmas morning."

Kris approached his crew of caribou and walked in front of them, looking each one of them in the eyes as he passed by. "The nine of you are the finest reindeer in the entire North

Pole. Each of you were selected, by name, for this Christmas Eve's trip. You have been blessed with the strength and stamina needed to take on the harsh winter elements around the world. The mission is so demanding, only those appointed by God himself can be considered for such a task."

"But it's not just your strength alone that makes you great individuals. You have proven yourselves, not only as great athletes, but as leaders and stewards to your fellow beings. Everyone here has witnessed the sacrifices you have made and can attest to just how critical you are to the entire operation. You have earned the respect of every animal in the North Pole, including the elves. And... you have also won my respect, as well."

The reindeer remained at attention for their master. They looked forward, without motion. But as for their friends and families, they all looked on with pride. Everyone in the North Pole was proud of their reindeer.

Kris returned to his spot in the center of the room. "I don't have to tell you that this year's journey will be more demanding than any other mission in history. I assure you that there are going to be some who will want us to fail. For many adults, Christmas Spirit is at an all-time low. But not in the children."

"That's where we come in. Tomorrow, we will be called to fulfill God's purpose. We've been anointed to continue the mission of gift giving, and with the Lord's favor, we will succeed. We will be successful in delivering those gifts, no matter what hurdles we may face along the way."

As Kris continued, the toyshop was completely silent, as the elves listened. Like the radio broadcasting days of old, everyone was tuned in. Pinky just sat at her window looking outward. She imagined the entire team flying through the night sky and making their deliveries.

Kris began to get excited, the more he spoke. "Right Here and Now, I claim victory for all of us! I am announcing triumph over the trip, and I am declaring a successful Christmas mission for all the children of the world! For tomorrow, when we take flight, we will not do so as eleven individuals. We will do so as brothers. And through our brotherhood, we will be victorious."

"It may not be easy. But then again, when has any great mission ever been so? I'm proud to be a part of this team. Each and every one of you has put your own wants and needs, second to that of what we have been asked to do. You are the best reindeer a Santa could ever ask for."

As Kris continued with his talk, families around the world were enjoying the early Christmas celebrations. Some were out for the evening, relishing school concerts and pageants, while others were traveling from home to home singing carols to their neighbors. Still, others were finishing up their seasonal shopping, and were wrapping gifts for their loved ones.

Kris stood quietly for a moment as he looked at his crew. "I thank all of you. Mrs. Claus thanks you. The elves thank you, and everyone at the North Pole appreciates you. But not only us... Gloria thanks you, and Justin thanks you. Mario and Cindy thank you. Every child on earth thanks you for your service, and they are praying for you to remain well as we deliver those precious gifts to them. They're all good children and all deserve to experience the joys of Christmas morning. They deserve to know just how loved they are. For us, we know that those gifts will fill their tiny hearts with the same joys that Jesus felt when he received those gifts. What better mission could there be but to bring happiness to the world?"

During that moment, Patrick saw a vision of his son and daughter as they arrived home to be with Katie. He saw Katie's delight as the grandchildren rushed up to the house and hugged her, as she met them at the door. Patrick felt that same uneasiness he had experienced earlier and understood that the vision he saw was reflecting what was happening back at home.

Kris grew quiet and smiled. Patrick was moved by his words of encouragement and began clapping. John Dreiling followed his lead and soon all the animals throughout the ranch began cheering loudly for their Santa. Pinky wiped the tears from her eyes as she looked out her window. She dried her cheeks and smiled for her husband. A lauded roar echoed throughout the workshop as the elves found the energy they needed to finish the remainder of the toys for this season.

Kris looked over to Patrick and winked. He knew, that without him, this year could have been compromised, and for that, Patrick was his hero.

Looking around one final time to his reindeer, Kris smiled, overwhelmed with respect and love for the caribou. "Merry Christmas. I love you guys."

CHAPTER TEN

It was the dawn of Christmas Eve. For everyone living at the North Pole, the day before Christmas was the quietest forenoon of the year. Not a single elf walked the streets. There were no merchants or bakeries opened, and there was no-one awake to patrol the streets. The elves had finished their year of toy making and could all be found sleeping soundly in their beds, away from the hustle and bustle of the workshop.

The morning of Christmas Eve began the very first day after all the gifts of the world had been completed. Not a single wish letter remained to be read. Not one toy sat in the shop unfinished. There were no more gifts to wrap and the candy factory was officially closed for the year. The season was over. It was the tradition at the North Pole that every elf be allowed to sleep in, the day before Christmas. For that day, there was an important event, cherished by the residents of the land. Today, they would gather and send their beloved Santa on his way to deliver the children's presents.

As for Patrick Wolf, Christmas Eve marked his final day at the North Pole, nearly fulfilling his obligation and returning home to Katie. Patrick awoke from his sleep a renewed man. Just one month prior, Patrick was on course to losing faith in life, because he had lost faith in himself. There were no words to how grateful he was for the opportunity to find Kris that winter morning. Wolf had been given a second chance at life. Patrick's experience with Kris, Pinky, Mr. Dreiling, and all of the elves, was magical and life fulfilling. Patrick had found new ambition for himself and more importantly, a new hope for Christmas. Patrick accepted the challenge given to him by Kris and had found victory by renewing his mind. He was allowed a second chance to mature into the person that God had meant for him to become.

The only thing that stood between Patrick and home was his flight around the earth. Today, all of the endless workouts and training were going to be put to one final test. Patrick was confident that after the journey was completed, after he and Kris were done delivering the presents to the world, that this year would go down in history. This Christmas would always be remembered as the year Patrick Wolf came to town. This year was going to be Wolf's Christmas. Patrick was indeed ready.

As he climbed out of bed for the last time, Mr. Wolf made sure to leave his quarters as clean as he found it, just a short few weeks ago. He grabbed his father's ring off the night stand and placed it on his finger. Thanking his dad for being with him in spirit throughout the past month, he was confident that his father was watching.

Entering the living room, Patrick decided to thank Pinky and Kris and John Dreiling, by preparing a down home mid-west breakfast for all of them, as a small token for everything they had done for him. Although he would not be returning, he now considered them friends for the rest of time.

Patrick went to the fridge and grabbed the essential items needed to make Denver styled omelets and French toast. As everyone at the ranch slept, Patrick was at work, preparing a country meal for his loved ones.

Soon, the aroma of breakfast filled the Claus home. Stirring Kris and Pinky awake, they came in to join Patrick in the kitchen. Not far behind them, John Dreiling entered the home to wish Patrick and Kris well on their journey. Patrick and the Clauses asked John to have breakfast with them and they refused to take no as an answer. Mr. Dreiling accepted the kind offer. He was more than honored to be asked to be part of this year's breakfast. The quartet of friends sat together, for one final morning, and enjoyed each other's company. They had grown close to each other. This morning, they were more than just friends. Today, they broke bread with one another, as a family.

The dining room echoed with sincere laughter. Patrick had never shared such a bonding in his entire life. Over the past few weeks he had made three friends that he would cherish beyond the days of his life. Madcap gestures were freely expressed amongst everyone in the home. Behind every story and every farce was the attempt to share love to each other, ignoring the angst that was silently stalking the four of them, each in their own unique way.

Once the breakfast morsels were finished and the last of the orange juice had been swallowed, Mr. Dreiling stood from the table to say his formal farewells. He needed to dash away and grab the reindeer.

Although he would be there to send them off, he decided to get the sappy goodbyes out of the way, as the celebration would probably be too chaotic to do it appropriately at that time.

Patrick stood behind his friend and rapidly reached out his hand to him. His palm shaking, through the assistance of mixed emotions, John swung his hand towards him and gripped Patrick firmly.

Patrick held back the tears. He was going to miss his new friend very much. "Thank you, John. I will never forget you."

John felt the sincerity from Patrick's words. Not one to often express emotions, John smiled at his new brother and pulled him in for a hug. "Good luck brother. Until we meet again, take care of yourself. Oh, and please send my love to Katie."

John then looked over to Kris and shook his hand as he placed his other upon his master's shoulder. With an uncontrollable smile, the two shared a laugh together. There were no other words that needed to be said between the two souls, beyond the shared merriment. After several decades together, the laughter between them was a sign of respect, that words would simply not be able to express.

John then gave Pinky a hug and a kiss and turned to walk out the door. Before making his exit, he turned to look back at the remaining party, wished them a Merry Christmas and a God Speed, and disappeared into the dark morning air.

Kris looked around the table to his wife and then over to Patrick. "How would you like to go on a trip, today?"

Patrick returned a nod to Kris with confidence. He was indeed ready to fly. Never in his life had Mr. Wolf been more prepared to travel the world. Second only to his wife and children, Patrick's time at the North Pole had proven to be the most important learning event he had ever experienced.

There was not one soul at the North Pole that did not recognize the sacrifices of Patrick Wolf. He had found himself in a mysterious land and had been asked to fulfill a task that was so impossible, it was actually considered folklore to the rest of the planet's inhabitants.

Pinky approached Patrick to embrace him and thank him for everything he had done for them. She was so grateful to him for literally giving up his life to help Kris on this very day.

Pinky held him tightly in sincere gratitude. "Thank you for being our guest this year. Kris and I will never forget this, and you will forever be a friend to everyone here."

Pinky then kissed Patrick on the cheek. Stepping back she clapped her hands in excitement. "We have something for you to take along on the trip."

Patrick had received nothing but loving kindness from Pinky and Kris. He did not feel worthy of being presented with anymore graciousness from his hosts.

Pinky walked over to a couple doors along the wall and swung them open. Hanging Inside the closet hung Kris's entire holiday wardrobe. Patrick looked upon the uniforms in awe, just like he used to do, back when he was a young Wolf.

Pinky stepped inside the room and grabbed one of the uniforms, hanging in plastic next to Santa's famous gear. She pulled it from its hanger and reattached it to a hook on the door so that she could present it to Patrick. Kris rubbed his hands with excitement as he and Patrick watched Pinky unveil the Uniform. As she pulled the plastic upward, a dark green suit appeared before them.

As Patrick stood silently, looking at his flight suit, he clapped his hands as an expression of a job well done. Pinky blushed with embarrassment and nervously responded with a curtsy to the men. Patrick was beyond appreciative. He was struck silent as his heart overflowed with appreciation.

Very happy that Patrick loved his gift, Pinky spoke to him. "It's not much. We only had a couple weeks to make it."

Patrick loved everything about his new suit. He responded to the Clauses to reassure them. "It's perfect."

Patrick's uniform was tailored by his new friends, specifically for him, and that was all he needed to be happy. The flight suit was a dark emerald green, one of Patrick's favorite colors. From his broad shoulders, down to his knees, the coat was designed with fur and leather to keep the Icy cold elements from damaging his flesh. The hat matched his coat, made from the same furs and leathers. The vest and suit pants were all leather, and attached to a pair of black leather combat boots, matching the pants. To accessorize the entire flight suit, the belt and gloves were decked out in leather and lined with fur. The buckle that fastened to his belt was pure silver and glowed from the lights in the room. This was the most modern looking Santa suit that Patrick had ever seen. He fell in love with it instantly.

Kris put his hands around Pinky with excitement. "Yes indeed! You outdid yourself on this one, baby. I'm actually kind of jealous!"

Pinky laughed loudly and kissed her husband on the cheek. She then reached in and pulled out a second uniform very much like the one that was tailored for Patrick. Only this one was made with Santa's traditional reds. Blushing, Kris wrapped his arms around Pinky and gave her a huge smooch.

Pinky was delighted and felt the Christmas spirit fill their home. "Merry Christmas, Patrick."

Then, spying the clock on the wall, Pinky widened her eyes as she felt that the time had slipped away from them. "Well boys, you had both better get dressed so we can send you off!"

Pinky smiled at the two and then left the room, leaving them to put on their uniforms. Once the men had taken time to admire themselves in the mirror, Pinky re-entered the room wearing her brand new Mrs. Claus uniform, matching Kris's perfectly.

Smiling from ear to ear at such a wonderful sight, Pinky was elated. "You both look so handsome!"

Kris was a smart and loving husband, so he wasted no time in returning the compliment. "And you look very beautiful, my love."

Patrick looked at his two dates and inquired of them. "So what's next? How do we do this?"

Pinky walked up to Patrick and licked her tissue. She then cleaned off the corner of his mouth, as she responded to his question. "Well... Before you all can go soaring around the big-wide-world, everyone will want to say a quick thank you and goodbye, and see you both off."

Mr. Wolf and the Clauses were ready. As they left the home, they approached the front drive, where John Dreiling stood waiting for them, with the sleigh and the team of reindeer. The sleigh was white with mother of pearl and lined with gold trimmings. The team of reindeer dawned with beautiful black leather harnesses with golden bells. John was very impressed at the sight of his friends. Placing his hands on his hips, John gave the handsome crew a whistle.

John then shook his head and thought about how far they had come as a team. "Wow! Don't you guys look sharp! Come on, let's get you to your party and get this ball rolling!"

Kris escorted Pinky to the sleigh and helped her into the rear of the rig. He then climbed up and sat next to her. Once they were comfortable, John and Patrick climbed on board, towards the front. John then took the reins and gave the command to Rudolf to move ahead. The thirteen of them began to slide forward, across the snow, leaving the ranch behind them. Just a short trek across the countryside, they headed towards the workshop.

As they left the ranch, Patrick looked back one last time to forever ingrain the memory of the farm, and all its facilities into his head. He hoped that after his return home, that he would not ever forget his time here. Over the hill and through the dim twilight, the Workshop came into view. As they drew closer down the quiet path, the rest of the city was gathering. The elves were taking their places to see Patrick and Santa and to wish them well before the launch.

Kris put his arm around Pinky's shoulder and drew her closer to him. Pinky had been with Kris through many Christmases, and with each passing year she grew more worrisome for the well-being of her husband. Most years, Kris returned with stories of wonder and magic, but as time passed, added stories of the hatred between the people seemed to dilute the tales. She wished she could join him on his trip, but both knew that she was simply not built to survive the elements he would face along the way. Although Christmas was the most important day of the year to all mankind, Pinky wished he could just stay home where it was safe.

Drawing closer to the heart of the city, John pointed out many landmarks along the way. He told stories about each of them, and how they had an impact on the North Pole. John, a quiet man in nature, loved his friends from the arctic region and loved to tell the stories that made up their culture.

Upon reaching the back side of the workshop, the air of the quiet country side became saturated with the joyous sounds of elves. The workshop was all that stood between the sleigh and a galaxy of excited toy-makers. The doors opened to the shop and Rudolf guided everyone inside where they would make the final preparations for the flight, and where they would stage their appearance to the North Pole residents.

Passing through the quiet workshop, Patrick looked around where he was flooded with the memories he had created with his newly found friends. The trip had not yet begun, and already he didn't want this day to end. Mr. Wolf had made so many friends and learned so much about the North Pole culture that he felt like a family member with everyone he had the privilege to meet.

Patrick placed his arm over his seat and turned to look at the others. "Thank you, guys. I will never forget this."

Kris took his free hand and placed it on Patrick's arm.

Even though Patrick was eager to return home, he didn't want his time to end. "Let's make a promise to each other that even after I go home, that we will remain friends for the rest of our lives. Maybe next Christmas I can even introduce Katie to you when you make your way through."

Pinky smiled to Patrick and wiped a few new tears from her eyes. Pinky loved a good story about friendship and indeed felt a strong brotherhood between the three men. John Dreiling nodded, and from under his breath, agreed with the three.

Kris then squeezed his arm and patted him as he leaned back into his chair. "Well said, Patrick. We will indeed remain friends."

Once through to the other side of the workshop, they came to the exit doors where they were met by several elves. They were there to help go over the final checklist and orchestrate the beginning of the celebration. The sled came to a stop and John and Kris climbed from the sled and began talking to the elves. The elves handed their master the flight plan and discussed the route of flight, as well as the global weather patterns. They also briefed Santa with a few concerns they had for them, issues they wanted them to be aware of along their way.

The sounds of the cheering, just beyond the doors, created butterflies in Patrick's stomach. Thoughts of the worldly trip began to catch up with him as well as reservations and doubts. Patrick had been waiting for this very moment, since coming to the realization that he was at the North Pole. He had hoped for this day his entire life. He had exceeded the expectations of everyone through his commitment to help Kris. But even though Patrick had accomplished all the tasks that were thrust upon him, he still had reservations that he would be any help on this eve's journey around the world.

Sensing his thoughts, Pinky decided to keep his mind off the trip by keeping him occupied from himself. She leaned forward to him. "This is my favorite part of Christmas Eve. As soon as those doors open, you are going to experience what it's like to be a rock 'n roll star."

Patrick heard Pinky's words and looked back at her as he sighed.

After all that needed to be said had been discussed between the dispatchers, John and Kris returned to the sleigh and took their seats. All of the elves wished them God Speed and a very Merry Christmas. They then stood back from the rig, making way for them. Two of the elves took their place in front of the doors and then waited for their leader's command.

Kris drew Mrs. Claus in closer and kissed her on the lips. He then looked up at Patrick and laughed. "Patrick, are you ready to see something amazing today?"

Patrick turned forward and let out a large breath to calm his remaining butterflies. "I'm Ready, Santa."

With that, Kris gripped Pinky's hand and then looked over at his elves and gave them the command to begin.

The ground crew's head elf gave his master a wink, raised the radio to his mouth, and then he made the official broadcast for the pageant to commence.

From behind the door barriers, a trumpet began to play, and the cheering of the elves instantly grew to a deafening roar. After the solo trumpeter was finished, the entire elf band joined in and played "We Wish You a Merry Christmas," the Clauses favorite song, preparing the crowd for the big moment. And as the music played, the ground crew waited for their cue. With each passing bar of music, the reindeer grew more and more restless, and the individuals in the sleigh prepared themselves to receive the enthusiastic elves. Just as soon as the timed moment came, the elves opened the doors, exposing everyone to the thousands of eager toy makers.

The Christmas lights that lit up the dark path came beaming through the doors, illuminating everyone on the sleigh. John called to his deer and at his command Rudolf led the way forward and together, the thirteen member promenade had begun. As they made their way from the toyshop and into the street, the elves stood to their feet. The crew was then greeted by an entire city of screaming colleagues and fans.

As they entered the procession, Patrick was amazed to see that everyone in the North Pole had gathered to wish them a safe Christmas journey. Patrick could not help but to wish that Katie could be there to witness this very moment with him. He just knew that there was no way she would believe all the stories that Patrick was going to tell her.

Everyone at the North Pole had worked hard to prepare for this year's Christmas. The annual parade was designed by the city residents as a surprise for Santa and Pinky, so that they could express their gratitude for them. The citizens of the North Pole were of all shapes and sizes. They respected

Santa and Pinky very much and considered them, not only as their employers, but friends. And, not only were the elves excited to see the Clauses but they wanted to see their new friend, Patrick, as well.

The Parade was a beautiful sight indeed. Candle lit paper bags aligned the street, giving the sleigh's path a gentle glow. Christmas lights danced in concert to the music. Fireworks towered high into the twilight sky, screaming upward and then exploding into blossoming flowers of light, flashing throughout the air like a lightning storm.

Making their way down the path, songs of the holiday echoed throughout the land. Patrick joined Santa and Mrs. Claus, as they made sure to wave to everyone they possibly could. They did not wish for one single soul to feel as if they had been overlooked. The Clauses knew every family living at the North Pole. They loved all of them so much and were appreciative for all their hard work. Both Santa and Mrs. Claus understood their importance to Christmas and the mission. They believed that their mission would simply be impossible without the help of their small, yet large family.

Once they reached the end of the path, the sleigh came to a stop upon a circular turntable. As the music continued and the crowd's cheering resumed, the platform below them began to turn slowly until the team faced the long path back towards the workshop. After they came to a stop and everything was in place, John stood from the driver's seat and climbed down from the rig, where he walked around to the passenger side of the sleigh.

Mrs. Claus embraced her husband for several moments and began to weep. Santa tried to comfort her as she cried with a broken heart. As they held each other, their falling tears became contagious and many of the elves began to weep as they watched on. She held her husband tightly. Once was satisfied, Santa helped her to her feet. She smiled at Santa and said a few private words to him. Santa took a handkerchief from his pocket and patted her eyes as she spoke. She then smiled at him and kissed him, after they were encouraged by the crowd around them. Then, turning, she waved to the crowd and climbed off the sleigh with the help of John Dreiling. She wanted to remain next to the sled and as close to her partner as long as she possibly could.

Santa made his way into the front of the sleigh and officially took his seat as Santa Claus. From within the army of toy-makers, the elves began to chant Santa's name over and over again, prompting Santa to give them a big wave. After recognition to his elves, with a wave of his hand and a hardy laugh, he signaled to John. John clapped his hands and the elves signaled for the Christmas gifts. From out of the crowd, a team of elves appeared, carrying Santa's bag of presents towards the sleigh. The bag's appearance was very large and it took all the strength of the elves to place it in the back of the rig, where Santa and Mrs. Claus sat just moments ago.

Patrick, John, and Santa helped the elves with the precious cargo and secured it tightly. Without the gifts, the mission would be useless, so they made sure there was no slack in the line. There could be no possible chance of losing that bag of toys along the way.

While everything was being secured, several of John Dreiling's crew made their way around the sleigh looking for any possible discrepancies that could lead to a breach of safety. And while part of the crew looked over the rig, the other half made their rounds to each of the reindeer, speaking to them and making sure they were in complete health and that there were no issues with their harnesses. Once the final crewmember was able to look over Rudolf's shiny nose, and was happy with his inspection, he walked over to the side and gave Santa the thumbs up.

There was nothing left to inspect. The entire rig, the dear team, and their pilots were ready to go. Mrs. Claus reached up to Santa and held his hand. The entire crew then gathered around with Mr. Dreiling. Santa looked over to Patrick and grabbed his hand as well. John climbed up on the rig once more and placed his hand on Patrick's shoulder. Once in place, everyone around the sleigh bowed their heads in prayer, led by Mr. Dreiling. Patrick looked down to his father's ring as he listened quietly. John thanked God for providing a safe journey to the crew, and thanked the lord for bringing Patrick to them this Christmas. As he prayed, the music slowly came to an end, and the roar of the crowd grew quiet, until the only sound that could be heard was that of the morning air. And as John continued, all of the Christmas lights grew dark until the only light remaining was from the candles along the path. After the prayer, Mrs. Claus kissed her Santa one final time and then threw a kiss to Patrick as he shook John Dreiling's hand. John wished the crew well and then took Mrs. Claus by the arm and escorted her to their seat.

For the first time in a year, the North Pole was dark and not a sound could be heard. Everyone watched intently for the big moment. Santa looked over to Patrick and smiled, "Are you ready, Mr. Wolf?"

Patrick sat back into his seat and checked his harness. He then looked up and nodded with a smile. "Yes Santa. Let's do this."

So happy for his friend, Santa smiled back to him. "Merry Christmas, Patrick. You deserve this."

Patrick placed his hand on Santa's and gripped tightly. "Merry Christmas, Santa."

The two looked forward, down the darkened path, until Santa felt the time was right. In the silence, Patrick grabbed his ring and just held it tightly.

Santa then shouted to Rudolf and gave the order for the entire land to hear. "Now, Dasher! Now, Dancer! Now, Prancer and Vixen! On, Comet! On, Cupid! On Donner and

Blitzen! To the top of the rooftops! To the top of the walls! Now dash away! Dash away! Dash away, all!"

Suddenly, musical bells began to ring from out of the darkness. The Bell Choir Army began to play. Stretched along the candlelit runway, one thousand uniformed elves stood at attention with bells in their hands. And with the bursting motions of their arms, the bell army began to play loudly, signaling to the crowd that the time had come.

From out of the darkness, Rudolf's nose shone brightly, providing light around them. The crowd began to grow unsettled as they impatiently watched on for the big moment.

Santa patted Patrick's leg and looked over to Mrs. Claus, winking in her direction. He then looked forward, and with a great shout, clamored "Merry Christmas to all, and to all, a Good Night!"

With a crack of the reins, Patrick, Santa and the reindeer raced back up the runway, gaining speed as they passed by the elves, erupting with a blast of mightily roars. John Dreiling held Mrs. Claus as she attempted to hold back her tears, watching her husband disappear into the darkness.

The team rocketed down the path, drawing closer and closer to the workshop. As Patrick's eyes grew wider, Santa laughed with excitement. They raced along the path until suddenly, the sleigh lifted off the ground and they darted into the sky, just missing the colossal workshop building. As the team sped away from the crowd, their fan-filled screams and whistles faded away, until the only sounds remaining were from the rushing winds and the jingling of the bells. Faster than the speed of sound, the crew made their way towards Russia, leaving their loved ones far behind them.

CHAPTER ELEVEN

S peeding through the sky, Santa and Patrick went to work quickly in preparations of their first stop. Patrick remembered what he had learned about the gift delivery process, and made sure not to cut any corners. He climbed onto the back of the seat and began sorting the gifts so that they could expedite each stop along the way.

The first stop would be the homes of Siberia, the most eastern region of Russia. Once across the Bering Sea, Santa pointed out the very first house on their itinerary, home to young Aldyn and Kara. He then told Patrick to hold onto something tightly. Although Patrick had proven himself successful during flight training, this would be the very first real life landing of many. Santa would not be able to waist *waste* precious time with gentle landings. The best way to get

Patrick's feet wet was going to be to dive in head first and get back up in the air as soon as they could.

The reindeer were veterans of the Christmas Eve journey. When Santa pointed out Aldyn and Kara's home, they knew exactly what to do. With a look around them for anything that would hinder the sled's performance, the deer checked carefully to make sure that their flight path was clear. The team then dove from the sky, darting directly towards the house. Patrick had not fallen from such a high altitude before. He held onto the sleigh tightly, strengthening his grip with every passing second of their rapid decline. Patrick was amazed at just how maneuverable the caribou and the sleigh were. Without any effort at all, the sled pulled out of its descent, straight into a barrel-type-roll, and came out perfectly level for their first landing.

Santa brought the sleigh to a full stop on the house top, without a hint of stress on the roof and without any loss of stability on the slippery snow covered shelter. Santa looked around to see Patrick, frozen solid with astonishment.

He laughed quietly as he patted Patrick's gloves, trying to break him from his state of awe. "Watch and learn my friend. I'll run for a while and then we'll let you start house diving when you feel that you are ready. Now if you will... hand me the first bag, please."

Patrick placed the very first bag of gifts into Santa's hands. Then he sat back and watched the iconic holiday figure make his dash to the first chimney of the year. Santa waved his hands over the flue and then simply jumped down the opening, deep into the home. Once at the bottom of the fireplace, Santa took his first steps into the living room, where a beautifully decorated fir tree stood. Santa pulled out the presents for Aldyn and Kara and placed them gently under the tree, alongside an assortment of packages from the children's parents. Santa then stood to his feet and looked around to find that this year, they had prepared a single cookie and a glass of milk for him. Without hesitation, Santa enjoyed the first treat of the evening. He then looked around to make sure that everything was in place, just like it had been before his arrival. Then with a nod, he darted back up the chimney, back to the sleigh. After he was safely out of the house and back at the rig, the fireplace magically reignited, and the team took off for the next house.

What seemed like three minutes to Santa, felt more like a fraction of a second to Patrick. The reindeer guided the sleigh back into the night sky and over to the next house. And, just as quickly as they fulfilled the first home, Santa leaped from the sled, into the chimney, and then back out again, launching back into the air with his crew within a matter of seconds.

Throughout all of Siberia, everything ran smoothly. With each stop, Patrick felt like Santa's pupil, learning everything he could about the gift delivery operation. Little by little, Santa allowed his assistant to help out more and more. And by the time they reached the end of their stay in Siberia, Patrick felt confident that he could run solo for a while, giving Santa a breather.

From the arctic cool climate of northern Russia, Santa and Patrick climbed in altitude and made their way down south, on a path across the Pacific Ocean, to Papua New Guinea, over towards Australia, and then up to Indonesia. By the time the team had reached Japan, Patrick was ready to take over the sled and make the deliveries, completely on his own. Santa was more than eager to see what Patrick could do. He leaned back in the sleigh and handed the reins over to Patrick, giving him control. The reindeer looked at each other, unsure whether to be nervous or excited about the change of command, but they pressed on, as there was no time for hesitation.

Patrick felt confident in his ability to land the rig safely. He had practiced hundreds of landings back at the North Pole, and had become very assure of himself. He found the first house of Japan and commanded the deer to make a diving approach towards the home. Knowing perfectly well that the caribou were in charge of the craft's performance, Patrick could only believe that he could guild the deer safely on his first solo landing. The incoming home grew closer, and with each passing second, Patrick noticed that Santa began clutching the rig. Patrick laughed as he brought the sleigh to a perfect stop on top of the house.

With a sigh of relief, Santa handed Patrick his bag of gifts and chuckled at Wolf's self-assurance. Patrick accepted the pouch, but before he could take it from Santa's grip, Santa wanted to give him a quick instruction. "Remember, on this evening you too, have been anointed with my powers. Just believe in yourself. Don't doubt. Then, be ready to make the leap inside, as fast as you can."

Patrick nodded rapidly and took the bag into his grasp. He then walked to the side of the sleigh, took a deep breath, and waved his hand out in front of him. Just like Santa had taught him, a supernatural opening appeared in front of him. Patrick wasted no time in leaping deep into the home. Once inside, he looked around for where the family had placed their decorations. Although Ms. Joyance covered many of the worldly traditions in her class, Patrick was not completely sure what to expect. But, low and behold, the family had actually sat out a tree in their home. Patrick smiled and went right away into Santa mode, delivering the children's gifts, and then making his way back outside. Once back on top of the roof, Santa smiled brightly and clapped in approval over Patrick's performance. Patrick climbed on board and looked over to Santa with pride as he grabbed the gear from Santa. He then cracked the reins and the team was on to the next home.

As they flew into the night sky, Patrick spoke to Santa. "I didn't see any cookies!"

Santa laughed with a shrug of his shoulders.

Back in the air, Santa grabbed the radio and did a routine check with Dispatch, who had been watching over them from back at the North Pole. From time to time, Santa felt that it was important to get fresh weather updates, as well as, discussing any concerns that dispatch felt was important to talk about. He didn't want any sudden surprises to sneak up on them along the way. He wanted his team to be prepared for what was ahead of them at any given point of the trip. Dispatch informed Santa and Patrick that the biggest weather factor was the winter storm forming over the United States, just like they had expected. Santa and the elves had been watching that system for a couple weeks and found no surprise in its presence.

After discussing the weather, Santa asked if there was anything for them as far as the Middle-East. Dispatch informed them that there had been some military activity over Kabul, before nightfall, but at the moment, everything seemed to be calm. Dispatch warned them to take caution over the city as at any time, things could become active again. Santa made sure that Patrick understood everything that had just been explained to them. He then thanked dispatch for the information, and they continued on their journey. Santa then took the radio and placed it securely on the dash.

As Patrick, Santa, and the reindeer made deliveries across China and Asia, Patrick was feeling quite confident in their accomplishments. Other than his family, Patrick had never been so proud in his entire life.

Patrick was starting to feel confident in himself. "I thought you said this was going to be hard!"

Santa found the humor in what Patrick had said and laughed loudly. Up to this point, there were few instances that brought any concern to the team. However, Santa knew that soon, things were probable to change quite rapidly, as those changes seemed to be the norm for them during the last several decades.

Santa laughed with Patrick. "You're doing great!"

As the two joked with each other, Santa knew that the next country was Afghanistan, where the city of Kabul resided, and where war had been taking place for a long time.

Santa's smile ran away from him and he thought about what was to come. He decided that now was the time to prepare. "Remember Kabul, the city where dispatch reported the military disturbance?"

Patrick remembered the conversations on Kabul very well. And the look on his face from the very mention of the city, made that very apparent.

Santa looked Patrick into the eyes to be sure he understood what he was going to tell him. "Well, my friend, we're approaching Afghanistan right now. On my word, we're going to go radio silent and into stealth mode."

A little unsure of what to expect, Patrick gave Santa a nod and continued flying forward.

Santa did not delay, once Patrick acknowledged what he had said. "Good. In three, two, one..."

Suddenly, everything on the sleigh went black and silent. All the sleigh lights were diminished, and all electronics were switched off. Even the bells on the sleigh were dampened where they could no longer be heard by the most sensitive of ears.

Patrick was confident in Santa's abilities. He did not do anything that would hinder Santa's performance. In amazement, Santa continued visiting homes, just as he did prior to going stealth. The team dashed like lightning from home to home. Not a word was spoken, and not a single sound was made; yet, they performed without incident.

Only between cities, did Santa attempt to speak to Patrick, and it was kept short and to the point.

As they continued, they were unaware that North Pole Dispatch was attempting to make radio contact with the crew. Dispatch wanted to warn Santa of possible unfriendly activity in the city of Kabul.

Back at the pole, Dispatch tried to get a transmission with the sleigh and give them the details. Their inability to make contact worried them; however, they were not concerned for Santa's ability to make good decisions. Looking at their path and seeing that their last ping was on the boarder of Afghanistan, the communications specialists felt confident that Santa had gone into stealth mode purposely and not through any mistake. They placed their radios on the desks and then waited, quietly.

Santa was no stranger to Kabul and the turmoil that continuously dwelt there. He told Patrick that if anything should happen while they were there, and if he was to become unusually delayed, that Patrick should not wait for him, but should go and get back to the North Pole. Once Santa spoke to Patrick, the two dove from the sky and headed to the heart of town. From house to house the team flew, making sure not one gift was spared. As they grew closer to the end of the city, it almost seemed as if things were going so well, that they were actually picking up speed between each house. Just as Patrick felt comfortable that they would conquer Kabul without any issues, they suddenly found themselves surrounded by artillery fire.

Without hesitation, Santa turned on all electronics and immediately discontinued their stealth mode so that Patrick could call for assistance. From out of nowhere, deadly ammunition began flying past them. The crew was not sure they were the actual target in this round of fire, but they decided not to hang around to find out. Santa started flying tactical maneuvers in order to avoid being shot. At the same time, Santa continued with the mission, trying desperately to find a safe place to land, so they could deliver their presents to a nearby orphanage.

Patrick was afraid for his life. They needed those electronics; however, by powering them back up, they could now be tracked by the very people who were firing all around them. He had to rely on Santa's experience to get them through this moment safely.

Trying to stay calm, Patrick yelled out to his Master and asked him. "What are we going to do Santa?"

Santa pointed firmly to an unlit area, just behind the orphanage building. He chose that very area as their landing zone, so that they could deliver those presents to the kids.

Taking no chances, the reindeer successfully landed in the dark yard. Santa grabbed his bag, and hopped from the sleigh, and then darted into the building as quickly as he could. And just as fast as he entered the dark home, a screaming noise came piercing from the sky above them. Looking up with fear, Patrick saw an explosive hit the building with a powerful blast.

Patrick remembered the instructions that Santa gave to him, and immediately took the reins and commanded the reindeer to go. But before he could get the orders out of his mouth, a second explosion blew around them; scaring the reindeer and forcing them to hesitate. Patrick needed to get the sleigh off the ground and away from the danger. He stood and shouted to his team, trying to get their attention off of the chaos around them and back to the mission at hand.

After a couple shouts, Patrick managed to take their eyes away from the fiery blaze and back towards a dark area where they could safely launch. And just as Patrick raised the reins to command the team, from out of the burning building came Santa, carrying his bag over his back and a child in his arms. Patrick froze with amazement as he saw his hero approach the sleigh. Parts of Santa's suit were burning as he made every attempt to protect the young person. Santa hopped in the sled and ordered Patrick to go.

Patrick wasted no time and cracked the reins with force, launching the team into the sky. Once in the air, Patrick handed the reins to Santa, exchanging the leather straps for the child. And just as they picked up speed and left the fires behind them, they were spotted by enemy aircraft, and were immediately targeted to be fired upon.

Santa shouted to everyone on board. "Hold on to your assets! It's going to get a bit exciting around here!"

Santa instantly went into a barrel roll to avoid the screaming bullets, and then dove straight downward. After the dive, he made a one eighty degree turn and headed back towards the fiery inferno where they just launched. Flying low to the ground, they felt like they had just lost the fighters when they nearly ran head on with three attack helicopters that had been looking for them. They had been tracking them from the moment Santa turned on the rig's electronics.

Patrick saw the helicopters first and warned Santa to keep going forward to avoid being hit. Santa complied and darted towards a gap between the enemy aircraft and then continued on into the darkness. Approaching taller buildings, they increased their altitude and flew above them, only to find that the jet fighters were behind them still. The gunman in one of the aircraft painted the sled with his radar, locking his guns onto them to shoot them. The second he had them locked on his target, he flipped the trigger guard and prepared to fire.

When out of the night sky three jet fighters appeared and returned fire onto the attackers. Santa and Patrick were in the clear, after a little help from the friendly aircraft.

In shock and celebration, Patrick roared at the top of his lungs, "We made it!"

Just as soon as they were able to level out their sled and reach a modest speed, they were met by a United States helicopter. They came up beside the team, nearly metal to metal, and gave the signal to Santa. Knowing that the aircraft was friendly, Santa took the child from Patrick and reached his arms up, handing the young cargo over to the soldiers. With thumbs up, the helicopter rotated away from the sleigh, and the troops headed around, back into the night, with the child.

Patrick had believed they were on a secret mission so he was confused to see an American helicopter interact with them. "How in the world did those soldiers know that you needed help so quickly?"

Santa laughed and answered him, "Remember our NORAD talk? Sometimes it's good to have someone looking out for your well-being and ready to assist you in an emergency!"

Patrick felt relief at Santa's laughter but did not want to go through anything like that again. "Is that the last of those kinds of surprises?"

Santa wished he could promise him a smooth ride, but in reality, there was not one nation on earth that didn't have its share of problems. "Well, there's still Africa and Europe and the Americas. The night is still young my friend!"

With a thankful, yet nervous laugh, Santa shouted. "Enjoy it!"

Amazed that Santa was still breathing, Patrick looked over at him with concern. "How are you feeling?"

Santa brushed over his uniform with his hands. He found several areas of his flight suit that had been damaged in the flames. Tiny debris also left holes through the insulated fabrics.

Santa looked back over to Patrick with a look of, "that was a close one," on his face. "Well, my uniform has been better. I took a couple good slaps but will be okay."

As soon as the team reestablished radio contact with Dispatch, they were warned about the new military activity over Kabul. Santa, being a compassionate Claus and not wanting to make his elves feel stupid, thanked them and told them that they would keep their eyes peeled.

Dispatch then gave Santa an update on that rare winter storm over Chicago, armed with heavy snow and arctic winds.

Santa was very appreciative for the heads up. He knew the importance of Chicago and remembered that many wonderful kids lived in that city. He didn't want to fail the children of a Christmas so he was going to have to keep an eye on the storm's movement. He knew that to assure those kids their gifts, he was going to have to decide on the best way to attack it.

As the team continued west, Santa landed the sleigh for a moment in order to give everyone a quick break, so that they could compose themselves. After the reindeer inspected each other and looked over their armor, Santa released them to go get a drink from a nearby water reservoir. He then asked Patrick to walk with him for a moment.

Patrick looked around at the quiet air that surrounded them. "Where are we?"

Santa looked up from the reindeer and over to Patrick and unveiled the surprise. "We're just outside of Bethlehem. This is where it all started."

CHAPTER TWELVE

Bethlehem was very peaceful. Most of the city had finished their Christmas Eve celebrations and had retired for the evening. After the excitement they just experienced in Kabul, Bethlehem was going to be a much needed break.

Patrick was so honored that Santa decided to stop in Bethlehem. At this moment, his entire Santa Claus career came full circle, as he looked upon the city where Jesus was born. The two men sat for a moment. And as they rested, Santa began to feel a discomfort in his side and began to cough, trying to clear his lungs.

Patrick observed Santa's eyes at that moment. The look on Santa's face was not a casual expression but one of concern. However, Patrick knew that Santa had made this journey, each year for many years and was probably one of the most experienced aviators known to man. Patrick believed that if there was a problem, that Santa would have enough faith in him to tell him the truth.

Santa wanted Patrick to see the city of Bethlehem for himself. After clearing his lungs he spoke to his partner. "You see, Patrick, Christmas has never been about me, or you, or any of the elves, back at the shop. Christmas is about the birth of Jesus who came here to save us from our-selves. It was right here where the first gifts of Christmas were offered."

Santa didn't want to leave this very location without taking a moment to just bring the beautiful view all in. "It is God's wish that I continue that tradition, by giving gifts to the children around the world each Christmas. It's not about how big or expensive the gift is. It's not about one child being more important than another. It's only about spreading the love of God throughout the world. That's it."

Once he was comfortable again, Santa stood to his feet and gestured to Patrick to stay where he was. He then walked over to the sleigh and grabbed a few items before returning to where they were sitting.

Santa handed a sandwich to Patrick and continued with his thoughts. "Look back at your children of Ellinwood. Over the years they had become less engaged with you as Santa, but that doesn't mean your mission was any less important. If there is one thing I can say about Ellinwood, it is that even though the vision of Santa may have changed, the love of

Christmas is stronger there than ever. You were an important part of keeping Christmas alive in everyone that knew you. You were appointed and anointed by God to be Santa. You have successfully used your role as Santa to fulfill the wishes of God, in order to spread joy to everyone at home. If tomorrow, everyone stopped believing in me, I would still continue to be Santa. God created this position so that His work could be continued. No matter how crazy I come across, until God brings me home, it is my purpose to make sure we deliver those toys."

Patrick smiled and shed some tears of happiness. He realized that his many years as Santa were actually not spent in vain. He was more proud to be Santa than ever before.

Patrick laughed and wiped the tears from his cheeks and then tried to lighten the mood a bit. "So what do I tell the people who complain when I put up my Christmas lights too soon or leave them up too long? What words of wisdom do you have about that?"

Santa joined Patrick in the innocent laugh and made his best attempt in answering him the best he could. "Well... Christmas is about the birth of Jesus, who came to earth to save everyone. It would be a shame to limit a gift of that caliber to one day or even a single month's worth of time. I'm sure Jesus wouldn't mind being celebrated everyday of your life."

Smiling, Santa took Patrick by the hand and helped him to his feet. There was still half a globe of Christmas to deliver so if they were going to beat the sun rise, they were going to have to get on their way.

And just as fast as they had landed, everyone was back into the air, recuperated from their break and ready to tackle the rest of the evening.

Santa grabbed the radio and patched in with Dispatch. "Merry Christmas, Dispatch! We're back in the air and on our way. How's everything for the rest of the Eastern Hemisphere looking at the moment?"

Dispatch informed Santa that everything looked clear as far as weather, and for the moment, there were no more demonstrations or disturbances on their watch list.

As their time over Africa and Europe passed, Santa's cough remained steady but did not seem to raise any alarms. Over Italy, Patrick and Santa pressed on, leaping from house to house in record time. Coming to a stop, Patrick hopped off the sled and dashed into the home with his bag over his shoulder. Quietly, Patrick placed the bag on the floor and reached inside, pulling out a new bike. He delicately placed the bike next to the tree and turned to make his escape. Turning rapidly, he spotted a figure standing before him. It was little Antonio's father, with a cricket paddle in hand. Before Patrick could bring the man into focus, Antonio's dad swung the bat at him with all his might. And like a flash of lightning, Patrick dodged the bat and punched the man in the face, knocking him out cold. Looking down to make sure the home owner was still breathing, Patrick then looked at his fist in amazement, and then darted out from the house.

As Patrick and Santa finished up all of Europe, the two had a big laugh at the expense of Antonio's father.

As the team passed over Sweden and Norway, Santa's cough began to grow more and more uncontrollable. With each cough, Santa began holding his side. Patrick had observed every cough, and through every hack and bark from his captain, he had to maintain control of the reins and pilot the rig so that Santa could try and relax.

Patrick's concerns began to speak to him, warning him to stop the mission and have Santa checked out. Patrick whistled loudly to the caribou and then looked over to Santa. "I'm going to stop this sleigh! You don't look so good right now!"

Patrick radioed in to Dispatch to inform them that they were going to take an unscheduled break over Keflavik Iceland. Once off the radio, Patrick commanded the deer to find a remote spot and land the rig.

Santa put his hands over his face. He didn't want to be the one who would stop the progression of this very important trip. Amazingly, though, they were well ahead of schedule and had plenty of time for the stop. Santa knew he wasn't as well as he should be. He was aware of the coughing, and he was also aware of the stinging in his side.

The only thing Patrick could think about was that his partner's suit had been severely damaged from the explosion in Kabul. Maybe his uniform was not providing enough protection to his body from the extremely cold temperatures, causing the developing cough. Patrick wanted to look Santa over and maybe bring in a new uniform, as well as medical assistance.

As soon as the deer came to a stop, Patrick leaned over to Santa to see what needed to be done to stop his fits. Although he was not having any issues with flying the sleigh, this entire evening was completely new territory to Patrick. He didn't want to fail at helping Santa complete his mission. He wanted to be remembered as the man who helped Santa deliver the gifts to the children, and not the one who procrastinated in getting Santa the help he needed. For the first time, he completely understood what Santa had been speaking about, with this mission. This had been very demanding on the both of them, more that he had ever imagined. Patrick was brought to the North Pole to assist Santa on his trip, and Patrick was going to make sure that his help was not given arrogantly.

Luckily, for Patrick, the chaos of the Middle Eastern countries was over with, and he felt that, even though there was still a major storm approaching, that they were now on a downhill slope to victory. Patrick was confident that this short stop would be what they needed.

As Patrick looked his partner over, Santa again started to cough roughly. Rocking back and forth, he tried desperately to relieve whatever was developing inside, so that he could breathe again. At this point, however, both men knew that the fits were more than just a simple cold setting in.

Patrick looked Santa directly in the eyes and asked him. "How are you doing buddy? Tell me the truth too!"

Santa was going to have to except the fact that there was a problem and then address it. "It sounds bad and it's feeling bad too. I'm not going to lie; I think it was from Kabul. Something during that explosion hit me and went through my coat, smacking me pretty hard."

Santa had Patrick grab the first aid kit where he found some cough and flu liquids. Patrick also looked over the wounded area on Santa's side. As he explored the area he saw that Santa had been hit by burning shrapnel, directly from the explosion. He also saw that Santa had been cut from the debris. Patrick stopped and stared at the opening, unsure what to do or say. Fear sat over him as he tried to think of what needed to be done and how his next move could affect the success of the mission. Finally, Patrick knew that Santa would want to know if anything was wrong.

Patrick sat back and gave Santa his diagnosis. "You're wounded, Santa. When that plane dropped that explosion on the orphanage, you got hit by something and it broke the skin. I'm not a doctor and I'm not sure, just how bad this is, but you are going to need to have it closed up before we go any further."

Santa knew he was injured. He saw the blood early on. He shut his eyes and sighed. Just as soon as the air passed through his mouth, he started coughing once again, irritating the wound with each loud bark.

Reluctantly, he asked Patrick to bring in help. "Call dispatch and have them bring a medic. Lord knows, this isn't the first time I've had a little cut. Then once they get me stitched up, we'll be able to get on our way."

Patrick found some material in the back compartment and wrapped it around Santa's mouth to keep the cold air from making things worse. He then jumped into the sled and called dispatch for help. In a matter of moments, help arrived and the two medical elves approached Santa with a replacement coat and to look at his side. After studying the situation, they applied a pain killer to Santa's side and closed up the wound, allowing him to be somewhat active again. The medics were very concerned for their master and tried to convince Santa to return to the North Pole with them. Santa had never failed on his Christmas Eve mission and was not about to allow this year to be his first.

He informed the elves that he was in sure hands with Patrick. He also assured them that if he got any worse, he would then call it quits and return back to the North Pole. With reservations, the medics allowed it. They then helped

Santa into his new winter wear and returned back to the North Pole, leaving the team to continue their mission.

Patrick gave a quick walk around to the team of deer and assured them that their master was going to be fine. The caribou understood the words and touch of Patrick's hand on their faces as a sign that they would soon continue. The deer began to dig at the ground and nod their heads, eager to begin moving again.

Once Patrick was sure that Santa was secured and comfortable, He grabbed the radio and informed the North Pole that they were ready to depart. Just as soon as Dispatch gave the all clear, Patrick cracked the reins and the entire team darted back into the night sky to make their way across the Atlantic Ocean. Their next stop was in the Western Hemisphere, where Patrick's wife Katie, was making final preparations for Christmas morning, without any knowledge of her husband's return.

The rig raced across the water, stopping quickly at Greenland, than then making their way to the mainland of North America. Back in action, Santa helped navigate the trip, giving continuous guidance to Patrick and the deer team as they made their way south, through the eastern coasts, from Northern Canada, to the most southern point of South America. With each passing border and every countryside boundary, the team prepared for the winter storm that was just hitting Chicago and maturing over the entire Great Lakes region.

To give the winter storm time to pass, Santa spoke with Dispatch and informed them that they would be covering all of South America and Central America before heading back to the United States. After the decision to alter the flight plan was made, Santa guided the rig along the coastal waters, into the rain forests, and up through the mountainous regions of South America. Patrick had never visited anything below the earth's equator, so he made sure to take time and observe all of the beautiful wonders along the way.

Once in Central America, Santa made the request to the reindeer to do a flyover of the Mayan ruins in Guatemala. Still very well ahead of the flight schedule, Santa felt that it was important to take a moment and enjoy the things that made the earth so unique. They flew over the ancient ruins and enjoyed them silently, as they passed overhead. And then, just as fast as they arrived, they continued forward, and up through the country of Mexico and into the Peninsula of Baja California.

As soon as they reached the boarder of the United States, Santa looked over the flight plan again, as well as the weather. After a second to think, he told Patrick that the winter vortex they had been concerned about had unexpectedly stalled over Chicago. And, that with every passing moment; the great lakes were feeding the storm's strength causing it to spread rapidly towards the eastern region.

Throughout all of South and Central America, Patrick could see that Santa's coughing spells were beginning to settle, but he did not want to approach that type of storm unless it was the only way possible to finish the Christmas Eve mission.

Patrick decided to check in with his leader. "How are you doing Santa? Can we do anything to give us more time to let that storm pass?"

Santa thought it over and tried to make the best decision he could. "Dispatch and I have been watching the trends of that snow storm, and I believe that if we don't hit it soon, it will just grow larger and larger, forcing us to spend more time inside the cold vortex. In order to make our time in that storm as short as possible, we'll need to hit the northeast coast and hit it fast and hard."

Like a lightning bolt, they screamed across the Continental United States, towards Vermont, where they left off earlier in the trip, before heading south. While passing the Midwest, Patrick thought of Katie, knowing that for a moment he was only miles from his family back at home. He thought of her beauty, and wondered if she was still baking cookies for the grandchildren, as they would soon be asleep, dreaming of what Santa would bring them this coming Christmas morning. As he approached Kansas he looked down, in hopes to see the lights of Ellinwood. He tried to focus, but before he could find the hidden lights within the ocean of darkness, Santa pointed out the lightning from the giant storm, directly ahead of them.

Throughout the evening, they had passed many snow showers, but the size of this storm made Patrick feel very small and frail compared to the shear mass they were about to enter. Not only was the size of the storm a concern to everyone on board, but the system's strength reminded them of their mortality, compared to the act of God, developing before them.

The team wasted no time getting to the eastern side of the system and diving into the clouds like a piercing bullet, and getting to the first homes of the remainder of the year's journey. The sooner they could tackle the winter storm, the sooner Patrick would reach the end of the line and be returned home.

At this point, every member of the crew knew their role, flawlessly. They were continuously breaking speed records, delivering the gifts faster and faster with each stop.

The arctic winds had reached the United States. The past three weeks of working out in a barn had conditioned them all for this moment. They did not allow themselves to grow complacent or downgrade the severity of the storm in their minds. They had trained very hard for this night and were going to stay focused on the possible dangers that awaited them.

Once the entire Eastern Time zone had been delivered, the team turned and sprinted over the icy waters of Lake Michigan, making a beeline to the city of Chicago. The atmosphere was rough and jagged like giant rocky boulders. The sleigh and its crew of thirteen were tossed about from side to side. The winds were very strong and uncontrollable. At any given moment, and without any warning, the monstrous winds could push them higher into the sky or even thrust them closer to the ground. The turbulent sky began throwing Patrick and Santa from side to side, like they were tiny infants.

As they fought through the dangerous storm, Rudolf saw a communication tower drawing nearer; left completely dark after the winter wind damaged the aircraft warning lights towards the top. Rudolf had no choice but to make a sudden move to avoid hitting the giant metal structure. What was worse, there was no time to warn the rest of the crew.

With the sudden shift in direction, they nearly missed the dark tower. Santa felt the armrest of his seat strike his wound with force, knocking the wind out of him, and he instantly let out a scream. Completely out of breath and struggling to breathe, Santa could not make himself comfortable.

Everyone felt the force of the windy blows and knew where Santa's cries came from. The Caribou tried to stabilize the sled with all their experience and strength. Patrick looked over to his boss in fear, taking his concentration off the flight at hand. And, as he tried to maintain control of the sleigh, he also attempted to look Santa over.

For the second time on their trip, Patrick called out to the team of reindeer and then spoke to Santa about his intentions. "I'm going to land!"

Santa held himself tightly and looked straight ahead in both fear and anger. "No! Keep going! If we stop we may not get through this in time for morning!"

Patrick had lost all awareness of what was around them and was beginning to fear for their lives. From the moment, Mr. Christkind let out his scream, Patrick began to doubt his abilities to fly through the storm and deliver the children's presents in a safe manor.

Patrick, for the first time, was thinking of taking control and doing what he felt was right. "I've gotta land and have you looked at!"

Although he wanted desperately to continue, Santa understood how Patrick felt. On his first Christmas Eve, he too felt the same anxieties and allowed the voices in his head to convince him that the mission was impossible to finish. On that night, he too, quickly began to lose his situational awareness. Santa did not want Patrick to experience those same drawbacks. He was going to have to keep Patrick focused on the mission or all would be lost.

Santa looked at his side and gave it an honest inspection. "The bandage is still secured, and the wound is still closed."

Santa put his hand on the shoulder of Patrick as a meager attempt to calm him. "Stay focused and don't stop moving! Those kids need us! We can rest for a moment when we get to Mississippi! I promise!"

Patrick heard Santa and tried to keep his composure. The stag team, although roughed up from the storm, also knew what they had to do. They made their way to each and every home without resting, so that they could get out of the system as quickly as they could. It was important to keep moving so that they could get out of the winter weather and back to the clear skies as soon as possible.

Suddenly, Patrick's mind began to think about the moment that Santa, Mr. Dreiling, he, and the deer, all paraded by the workshop. He remembered the excitement shared by the team and city of elves. That moment was one of the proudest moments in his life. At that moment, he could see how important the entire Christmas Eve mission was. He thought about that moment in time, and the memory gave Patrick hope.

Out here in the night sky, they were all by themselves. There had been no cheering sections for the team this night. No one to give them words of encouragement or support. The purpose of their journey was to visit every child of the world as they slept. But even though they were alone in the night skies, their journey had a great purpose. Patrick knew that some of the greatest purposes in history were accomplished in solitude, just like the birth of baby Jesus.

Patrick and the team continued forward. They were afraid, but put their faith in God that he would guide them through until the end.

Soon, the bitter winds began to die down just slightly. To Patrick, although the shift was only moderate, it was not overlooked, and it helped to bring a second wind to the crew. By the time, the team reached the most southern tip of Illinois, the winds were near calm and the dangerous storm was behind them. The deer began to sprint forward in victory, and Patrick let out a yawp of excitement, throwing his fists into the air, claiming triumph for the entire team.

The warmer air was welcomed by everyone flying the ice-packed rig. Patrick called Dispatch to inform them that they had successfully delivered the presents to all the kids in Chicago, in spite of the weather. He also added that they were going to take a much needed break.

Patrick then yelled to Rudolph to make a landing so that they could rest. With a nod, Rudolf shifted downward, and they descended from the sky. Patrick looked over to Santa, and noticed that he was slumped over and unconscious. Calling out to his deer, they looked back to see the sudden change of circumstances and dove quickly, so Patrick could attend to Santa and see what had developed. The unexpectedly quick maneuver to avoid the tower had definitely injured Santa, on top of his already established wounds. After finding level ground for their landing, they touched down the craft as smoothly as they could. They did not want to bring any further injuries to their master.

Once they came to a stop, Patrick leaned over to Santa, just as he did back in Keflavik, to check on the health of his captain. Gently, yet with a little force, he grip Santa's arms and called his name. Santa opened his eyes, bringing relief to Patrick and the team.

Santa turned his head to Patrick and managed a smile. "You did a good job."

Patrick jumped from the sleigh, his cold joints aching, and ran over to the other side of the vehicle to check on Santa. As he made his way, Rudolph recognized the fear in Patrick's eyes. He then unhitched himself from the rig so that he could make his way over to his master to see what had happened. The rest of the deer, although concerned for Santa, stayed at their posts so that they would not get in the way.

Patrick reached inside of Santa's coat to check on the dressing. Everything was in place and, there was no blood to be found. He gently pressed on Santa's side, observing him for new injuries. The moment Patrick touched Santa's rib cage, however, his entire body tensed up and he let out a loud cry.

Patrick's eyes grew wide as he attempted to make Santa comfortable again. "You broke a rib, maybe more. You can't go any further. Not with all this."

Santa began to cry as Patrick pulled the plug. Although he had come close many times, he had never failed to deliver all of the presents before. Santa felt that he was the broken tool to this well-oiled machine, and it broke his heart. Patrick sat quietly with his friend, as he came to the understanding that the mission was over.

Santa cried, with a broken spirit. "I failed."

Patrick could not begin to understand the thoughts running through Santa's mind. Until a month ago, Patrick only considered the title of Santa as an important fictional character to the Christmas tradition, and at most, a parable to the story of Jesus's birth. In a very short moment in time, Patrick had learned more about the season than ever before. A revelation swept over Patrick, that if they were to terminate the trip at this point, that half of the children living on the North American continent would not receive a gift from Santa this year. Knowing that the mission was finished overwhelmed Patrick, and it broke his heart to know that Santa was immobilized.

CHAPTER THIRTEEN

Patrick watched quietly as Santa wept. In that moment in time, Patrick tried to think of anything he could to help Santa complete his mission. In the history of Santa, there had never been a failed mission. Patrick thought that if this was truly a God-given purpose, there would surely be a way to find success, even though, in the natural way of thinking, Santa's injury was a game stopper.

Out in front of the sleigh a grunt came from the team. Patrick heard the bleat and was instantly shocked, as he thought he actually understood what was said. Once again the grunt came from one of the caribou. Dancer was talking clearly to them.

Santa too, heard the suggestion and grew even more stressed. "No!"

Patrick clearly understood what Dancer was saying and began to think to himself about what had been suggested by the mighty stag.

After hearing what had been said, Patrick began nodding in agreement to Dancer's suggestion. He looked over to Santa, in shock, yet very excited. "I can do it, Santa. Let me go! I can deliver the rest of the gifts for you! I've basically been doing it since the explosion, anyway! Let me fly on. I promise that your mission will be completed successfully!"

Shaking his head, trying not to bring more pain to his side, Santa was in complete disagreement with the thought of Patrick finishing the trip on his own. "No! No! No! You don't even know what you are saying right now! You cannot do this, and I will not ask you to!"

Patrick was now the only hope for this Christmas Eve. There was no one else that had gone through the training like Santa and Patrick had endured. There was no elf or human that could come in and serve as an alternate Santa other than Patrick. Patrick was the only one capable to take over. Dancer knew this. The other caribou knew this. And, most of all, Mr. Christkind knew this.

Santa squinted in pain as he tried to explain his thoughts. "Patrick, my dear friend. I cannot ask you to do such a thing. You need to go home and return to your life with Katie."

Patrick did not understand. He had never been one to give up without at least trying first. "Who says I can't? I'll finish the trip and return home after that!"

Santa closed his eyes with guilt. Even if Patrick was to continue the trip and succeed, and even if Christmas was saved, failure would still come upon their mission. Santa would not be successful, no matter the decision that was made for the evening.

Santa sighed as he looked into Patrick's determined eyes. "Your body is going to expire tonight. Before Christmas morning, your old self is going to stop breathing, and it is going to pass away. If you go on ahead and do this, and you continue past Ellinwood, your body will expire, and you will not be able to ever go back home. You will not be able to return to Katie. That is something I cannot ask of you."

Patrick was confused. He understood how his body may pass but, here he was, standing in front of Santa with a new body. He was alive. How could this stop him from returning to Katie and to his life in Ellinwood?

Patrick was not going to give up, not with God as a witness. "So let it die then. Let me finish this, and then I'll go home."

Santa tried desperately to make Patrick understand. "You can't! Think about it! Once your body passes away you cannot return. Yes, physically, you could go home, but please think! The implications of you showing up after your death would do more damage to your wife than you can imagine. Her mind simply doesn't work that way. She will not be able to understand something so supernatural, and it will destroy her completely."

Santa was a true leader and did not want Patrick to lose his family because of him." I understand that you want to save Christmas. But I can't ask you to give up your life like this. I could not live with myself if I asked you to continue and give up your home, just to help me deliver a few presents."

Patrick looked over to the reindeer. He then looked at Santa and then to Rudolf, determined to find a resolution to their emergency. For the past several weeks, the people of the North Pole had taught Patrick about the importance of Christmas. And now he was being asked to leave it behind. Patrick simply could not see how doing the right thing could fail.

Patrick made his decision. "Rudolf, if I go on ahead, will you stay with Santa until help arrives?"

Rudolf nodded and grunted loudly. The entire team had made this journey many times, and Rudolf knew that the rest of the caribou would be more than capable of continuing without him. Santa watched on silently. He may not have been able to bring himself to ask Patrick to take over, but he knew that he was the only hope for the children.

Silence fell over everyone as they waited for an answer. Santa was in too much pain to wait much longer, and the sun would be rising soon. Patrick thought about the pain Katie would feel, this coming morning, if he did not return home. He was scared, and either way he decided, great pain would come to someone he loved, this Christmas.

With a shaky hand, Patrick leaned over and grabbed the radio to key it. "Dispatch, do you copy?"

Attempting to talk, Patrick found himself in tears. Clearing his throat, he was not exactly sure of what to do. "Dispatch, we need a medic to our location, please."

Patrick looked over to Santa as he sat in extreme pain. He watched the established leader of the North Pole cry silently.

Patrick re-keyed the radio. "Santa's down. We need a retrieval sled immediately. Santa will not be able to continue."

The radio was silent. Dispatch had never been asked to retrieve their master before and their pause was a clear sign of shock. The communication elves sat looking at each other.

Still not confident in himself, Patrick thought about it and then offered his plans. "I will continue the trip so I'll need all the assistance that I can get from you guys."

Dispatch responded to Patrick's information. They began scrambling to dispatch a recovery sleigh for Santa. They also began digging for all the charts of the Northern American continent, in order to be ready for any question that Patrick may ask.

Santa was relieved to hear that Patrick was going to continue, but he felt guilty for allowing such a circumstance to come to pass. Christmas might have been saved, but his mission to help Patrick return home had now failed. For Patrick's family, if he continued on pass his home, Christmas morning would forever be remembered as the day a loving husband and father died. The thought destroyed Santa inside.

Santa continued, trying to bring a little sense to his companion. "Please, no, Patrick. Your family needs you."

Patrick rested his face against Santa's forehead and kissed him as he held him close. He then spoke softly to him. "I love you, Santa."

Patrick smiled to his friend and patted him on top of his head. He then asked Rudolf to lie down on the ground as he helped Santa from the sleigh. Once he was safely out of the rig, Patrick guided Santa downward to sit with Rudolf. He positioned Santa so that he could cuddle up to his lead reindeer for comfort and warmth until the medics arrived. Patrick then thanked Rudolf for his help and made his way back to the team already beginning to prepare for launch.

Santa pleaded with him one last time. It was not too late. "Promise me, that when you reach Ellinwood, you'll stop. Promise me!"

Patrick looked at Santa without a word and then climbed on board the rig. He grabbed the reins, and wrapped them tightly around his hands. He paused for a silent prayer and cracked the reins, commanding the team to go. Donner and Blitzen darted forward leading the team, and as fast as a ray of light, they beamed into the night sky to finish delivering the presents to the boys and girls.

The evening air was much warmer than that of the frigid storm over the Great Lakes; however, now they were short two crucial team members. They were going to have to work much harder than before to finish the journey without any further hiccups.

Patrick called in to inform Dispatch that they were back in flight and made sure that help was on the way for Santa. Once informed of an arrival time to retrieve the others left behind, Patrick felt confident in continuing, knowing that Santa was in safe hands.

Everyone had trained for the impossible and was prepared to combat anything that was to come their way. From Mississippi to Louisiana, back up north to Minnesota and into the Prairie Provinces of Canada, Patrick and the deer pushed forward. With every passing home, Patrick thought of his wife, Katie. He knew that he would be arriving home very soon. Although he would not be allowed to be seen, he felt it a bit ironic that he was about to be the actual Santa Claus for everyone that he used to play Santa for.

Making their way back south, Patrick had found his pace and made each stop more and more proficient. Entering each home, either through the chimney or by supernatural forces, Patrick's training at the climbing wall had made entering a home much of an effortless event. Patrick made sure not to miss a single gift under the tree. He also made sure to take advantage of each and every milk and cookie tray that was presented to him. He knew that he would need to keep his energy up to sustain the velocity throughout the rest of the night.

Down through the Dakotas they pressed on, zigzagging across the countryside, continuing south through Nebraska until reaching Patrick's home state of Kansas. Still, amazingly ahead of schedule, Patrick decided that once they reached home, he would take his time to give one final look at his home town. He wanted to remember this night for the rest of his life.

Once reaching Kansas, time seemed to slow down for Patrick. His mind was on home, and he just wanted to be back there. Like the old saying, a watched pot never boils, Patrick was indeed watching intently for the lights of Ellinwood to appear.

As the minutes passed, Patrick grew nervous inside. In the grand scheme of time, the speeds that the team traveled were unfathomably quick. Faster than a single leap of a racing jackrabbit, Patrick and his team hurdled from house to house.

For the past few states, up until reaching his home turf, time seemed to come to a slow crawl. He had not felt so highly strung since the day of his wedding. The butterflies continued to flutter in his belly, until suddenly the team found themselves passing the city of Salina, where Patrick knew he was in familiar territory and just a stone's throw away from home.

From that moment, Patrick was able to use his scouting skills on Navigation and Orienteering and was finally able to find the lights of Ellinwood. His home town was faintly glowing into the evening sky, just beyond the edge of the plain's horizon. As they bounded each house, they progressed home. The glow of Ellinwood soon turned from a dim glimmer to hard points of light dancing in the humidity of the evening's winter air. And before they knew it, the final present had been delivered to the town of Claflin, Ellinwood's northerly next-door neighbor.

As they drew closer to the city limits of Ellinwood, Patrick eagerly shouted to the team to inform them that the upcoming municipal was his home town. Patrick looked down and witnessed the snow covered fields, glowing from the moonlight above. Limestone fence posts spread throughout the land, protruding through the snow, also lit up by the moon's light. The trees in the distance, growing along the countryside, looked like marshmallows under the snow. Finally, after a month's time, Patrick was back in Ellinwood.

He landed the sleigh on top of the local grain elevators, the community's highest point. He wanted to get a good look around the dark town. As with the cities prior, a few people were still making their way about the streets as the evening's celebrations were winding down. While most of the young residents were already asleep, most of the adults were finishing up their Christmas morning preparations in hopes that they too, would soon find their way to bed.

Living his entire life in Ellinwood, Patrick witnessed thousands of sunsets. He could only wish that he could have seen the evening's last light of day from this very location. As Patrick looked around his home town, he smiled as calmness grew throughout his body. The streets were lit with handmade Christmas ornaments, both new and old. Star and candle shaped decorations, as old as Patrick himself, enhanced the streets and sidewalks of the town. The lights bouncing off the wet streets made everything in sight glow, reflecting every color in the rainbow.

From out of the quiet evening air, Patrick began to hear singing. Unable to find where the voices were at, Patrick decided to find where the merriment was coming from. He called out to Donner and Blitzen and commanded them to continue. In order to not fall behind schedule, they would have to deliver the children's gifts while they sought after the singers.

Ellinwood was a small town with a small population, where everyone knew their neighbor, and where everyone within the countryside was considered a friend. By this time of the evening, Patrick completely understood how important it was to remain unnoticed while making his way through town.

With the extinguishing of each home's lights, Patrick hit the houses to deliver the presents. In this town, Patrick knew every child from his local Santa days. He placed every package under the tree with special care. He also took a little more time to answer the letters that the young ones had left for him, next to plates of cookies and glasses of milk. Patrick felt that by responding to each letter, he would be able to say everything he wished he would have, all those years before.

Patrick was so proud to be able to fulfill his Santa role and deliver the gifts to the children he had watched grow up, over the years. Although he dreamed of actually being a real life Santa, he never actually thought this night would come to be. Within moments, the southern half of Ellinwood was complete. As Patrick looked down the quiet Main Street, he spied the activity he had been keeping an ear out for. He could see carolers visiting their final home of the evening, which happened to be the home of one of his favorite Ellinwood residents. He then guided the team to a hidden place, just across the street, so that he could watch on. The merry carolers were knocking at the door of Dr. Law.

As one of the singers knocked at the door, the others in the small convoy climbed off their wagon and approached the home. With smiles on their chilled faces, they gathered at the steps of the house, rang the doorbell, and waited eagerly for the Law family to answer.

Everyone could see the Christmas lights shining dimly from the house windows, as beams of reds, yellows, greens and blues, leaped from the windows and on to the snow covered yard.

The faint lights were quickly replaced by brighter house lights, as the owners made their way to the front door. They turned on the porch light and opened their door to the unexpected visitors. Immediately, the carolers began to sing, "Joy to the World," filling their audience's home with the beautiful sounds of Christmas.

As Patrick watched on, from between two houses across the street, he hummed to himself. He watched the pleasantly surprised faces of the happy couple, as they stood in the doorway, singing to the music and smiling back at the carolers before them.

Dr. Law was once the town physician. He was an extremely kind gentleman and had a way with children, as well as, the adults of Ellinwood. As the carolers sang on, thoughts of Patrick's childhood began running through his head. He recalled Dr. Law in the doctor's office, pinching his nose, and making a funny squeaking sound with his lips.

Patrick tried hard not to laugh and draw attention, as he reminisced, but he freely smiled widely.

As the carolers sang to the Law's, it was obvious that this brief moment of music brought a sense of great happiness to the aging couple. They did not get out as much as they used to, so having guests was always an unexpected delight.

Up until this year, Patrick used to be one of the carolers. He and Katie used to travel with the small group of town friends and help bring joy to the unexpected audiences. The greatest part of caroling was to see the smiles on all of the faces, young and old. After a few holiday tunes, the carolers ended their serenade with, "We Wish You a Merry Christmas," and then waved to the Law's, exchanging many Merry Christmases and Happy New Years as they left, leaving their delighted neighbors behind. Patrick wanted to say hello, but remained in the dark space, and just took in the moment. The caribou began pawing at the ground, to remind Patrick of the time.

The Wolf's lived near the edge of Ellinwood, so Patrick made sure to visit every house in town first, making his home the final stop. He didn't want to feel rushed when he arrived. It was, indeed, the most special home he would visit during his entire Christmas Eve tour.

As Patrick reached the final neighborhood of Ellinwood, he looked down to the end of the street, where he immediately noticed that Patrick Juniors and Jena's vehicles were parked in the driveway. He was proud of his children for taking the time to be with Katie this Christmas. The feeling of pride for his family filled Patrick's heart. Here he was, standing on the street of his home, surrounded by the very best of friends that anyone could ask for, yet no-one could ever know that he was standing amongst them.

As the Caribou approached his home, he asked the team to land in the field behind a group of trees next to his house. He did not want to risk being discovered. Although, he and Santa had done very well at remaining stealthy throughout the evening, his own home would be the most crucial one of them all, and he did not want to make any mistakes.

As he grabbed Santa's bag of gifts for his grandchildren, he hopped off the sleigh and snuck up to the final home of Ellinwood, his home. Patrick was not surprised to see movement in the house, as he attempted to peak through the window, from behind the tree. Katie was never known to retire early, especially on Christmas Eve. It was her personal tradition to be sure that every gift under the tree was properly in place, and that each of her homemade stockings were packed full of small surprises. She would not sleep until her family was provided for on Christmas morning. Her favorite time of year was Christmas. For her to see the excitement of her children and grandchildren's faces on Christmas morning, was worth more to her than all the money in the world.

Patrick approached the window with care, as he did not want to be seen. As he drew closer, he could hear classic Christmas music coming from inside. The song playing was, Silent Night, Katie's favorite song. Many memories of their life together were created while Silent Night played. As Patrick looked inside he grew scared. He wanted nothing more than to see his wife. He wanted to go inside and hold her, and let her know that he was okay now. An overwhelming feeling of heartache filled Patrick's soul, as he remained hidden, and he began to shake.

Suddenly, Katie appeared to Patrick as she walked from the kitchen and into the living room. There, standing in front of the Christmas tree, was the most beautiful person that Patrick had ever known. She was more beautiful now than he could ever remember. She was holding something in her hands, looking upon it with a smile. But as she gazed at the object, tears began welling up in her eyes. She wept with both sorrow and with joy as she placed it amongst the many packages under the tree. Patrick watched Katie put their favorite photo of each other under the tree. For Katie, Christmas morning would not be the same unless a part of Patrick was there to join them as the family opened gifts together.

Patrick placed his hand over his mouth and began to cry as he wondered what was going through Katie's mind. It was obvious that she was thinking of Patrick and remembering her life with him. Patrick had never loved anyone as much as he loved Katie. He did not want her to feel any pain. All he wanted was to be her hero and go save her from her sadness.

As she stood back on her feet, she looked around the entire room, looking for any item that could possibly be out of place. When she was satisfied that Christmas morning was ready, she leaned over and took a cookie from the tiny plate that their grandchildren had left for Santa. She then quietly made her way into their bedroom, shutting off the lights behind her.

Patrick then entered the home and delivered the gifts for the grandchildren. He then sat down next to the plate of cookies, where he cherished each one of them, and finished off the glass of milk. He then took out a pen and wrote a letter to his family from Santa.

He had to write fast, as at any time, someone could come down the hallway. "Thank you so much for the milk and cookies. Chocolate chip has always been my favorite, and this year, they were very special. I hope you will enjoy the presents that the elves have made for you, and that you will get many years of enjoyment from them. These particular gifts were inspired by a new member of the North Pole, someone who loves you very much. Please don't be sad as Grandpa Wolf may no longer be with you in person. Instead, be assured that Papa is now with us, and will be helping us at the North Pole. He wanted me to tell you that he is proud of each and every one of you, and will always love you, especially

Nana Katie. Merry Christmas to you all, and God bless you! Love, Santa Claus."

After Patrick finished his letter to his family, he stood up from the table and looked around the room, just as Katie did moments before, looking for anything that may be out of place. With a heartbreaking smile, he removed the ring that his father gave to him many years ago. He took the ring and kissed it, and then placed it on top of the letter. He wanted Katie to know it was found. He believed that, once they read the letter and saw the ring, that just maybe, they would believe that he was somehow still alive. Patrick knew that he still had the freedom to call it quits, and that if he chose to do so, he would be returned to his body, making this Christmas morning one of the most blessed holidays ever. He knew he could remain at home. However, by doing so, the rest of the children would be the ones to suffer from his decision.

Patrick sighed under his breath and whispered, "I love you, Katie." He then turned reluctantly and left the home one last time.

With tears in his eyes, he quietly climbed into the sled and sat, looking up to the evening sky. He was not sure how to feel and needed to bring it to God.

In the presence of only his reindeer and the Lord, Patrick spoke silently. "God, I thank you for this opportunity to see Katie again. I know you are with me and want the very best for me, so I ask you to be with Katie and care for her always. I love her, and all I want is for her to be happy; yet, I believe you have sent me here to make sure Santa doesn't fail this evening. So I'm torn. I think if your will was for me to stay home, you'd make that clear by now, but here we are, sitting here with only me to finished the trip. I'm just going to give this to you and believe that you will see me through this and bring blessings from this moment. Thank you, God, and, Merry Christmas, Jesus."

Although Patrick wanted to return home to Katie, he felt that God's calling to complete the mission was even more important than returning home. He could only pray that God would reward him, and that Katie would find forgiveness for him.

He was not mad at Santa or with God. He was at peace with his decision to continue. However, Patrick definitely missed his wife. It didn't take long for Patrick to think about what Katie would say to him if she would have known why he decided to finish. He knew from the bottom of his heart that she would be proud of him for putting such an important purpose ahead of his own wants. Knowing that, Patrick smiled and continued on, delivering the gifts to the rest of the children.

Within a couple hours, Patrick and the reindeer had found themselves at the completion of the mission. The final package had been delivered and the last of the milk and cookies, eaten. Patrick informed the North Pole that

Christmas Eve had been accomplished and then he stood to his feet and applauded the remaining eight caribou for their help. He curled his arms upwards to flex his muscles and shouted out victoriously. The caribou joined Patrick in his excitement and began roaring Christmas merriment into the night sky.

Patrick had accomplished one of the most demanding tasks of his life. He helped provide Christmas to the world in one night, just like it had been written in the story books. Now, he wanted to get back to the North Pole so that he could deliver the news to Santa, who would be impatiently waiting for him, back at the ranch.

Patrick sat exhaustedly back in his seat and told the deer to return home. With that, Christmas Eve was over.

CHAPTER FOURTEEN

T he journey around the world had been the greatest adventure Patrick could ever imagine. Although he was excited to have taken part in such an honorable mission, his heart was heavy for those areas around the world less fortunate than what he had grown accustomed to, back at home. Deep inside, Patrick still wanted to return home to Katie and his children, but the decision had been made, and by now, he knew that he would no longer be able to return. As he approached the North Pole, he could not help but feel sorry for the news Katie would receive about his death.

Patrick could see the arrival lights to the North Pole and was immediately full of such relief that he began cheering in victory. The Reindeer, hearing the excitement in their driver's voice, mustered up the remaining of their durability and raced Patrick back to the sanctuary of the Ranch. All of the past evening's weight was lifted off Patrick's shoulders. The North Pole was the most beautiful sight he had ever seen.

As the sleigh started its approach to the landing zone, Patrick could see that there were more lights around the ranch than normal for this time of the evening. He could only hope that all this activity was a sure sign that Kris was safe and secure, and finally, in the loving arms of his wife.

The sleigh landed back at the North Pole with ease. Although the flight was now at an end, the evening was still in its final quarter. Patrick was now too cold and too tired to drive the sleigh. He gave up the reins and let the team of deer bring the sleigh to their final stop, back at the stables. Patrick looked around at the beautiful views that surrounded him. The toyshop and the buildings surrounding the plaza were still dark and lifeless, yet Patrick found glory in the stillness as he knew that everyone in the city was with their families.

Exhausted, Patrick could feel every emotion known to man rushing through his body, and he wasn't quite sure he knew how to take it all in.

With the weight of the world now off his shoulders, Patrick began to gasp for air and weep nearly uncontrollably. Tonight, Patrick observed the entire world before his very eyes. He saw the very Christmas that he could only dream about as a kid. He saw how the birth of one Child had changed the world forever, and for that he was the happiest man alive. On the other hand, Patrick witnessed the horrors of the Earth and would not be able to forget that Christmas around the world could only seem like a myth to those living in those areas.

He thought about his family and Katie again. How happy it made him feel, to see his children pass on the family traditions that he and Katie had instilled in them. He was so proud of them and only wished he would have been able to stay at home for good. He also remembered how beautiful Katie was this evening. He was relieved to know that she had not given up on life and not forgotten about him. He just wanted to hold her and kiss her. He wanted to protect her and to never let go of her again.

As the team entered the ranch, they were suddenly met by many of the stablemen as well as medical personnel. Hearing the approach of the jingling bells, they all stopped from their tasks at hand. They began to wave and applaud to Patrick and the team for a job very well done. This Christmas was Wolf's Christmas. He was a hero tonight.

The reindeer knew exactly where to go. They pulled up to the stables, where they were met by the stablemen, just like the hundreds of times before. Everyone went to work receiving the sleigh. Mr. John Dreiling waited patiently as Patrick remained in his seat for just a moment more. He needed a second so that he could come to grips with the night's experience, and to give a short prayer to God, thanking him for all of the evening's provision.

Everyone was excited that Patrick had finished the journey successfully. However, the return of the sleigh and the reindeer commanded that before anyone would be allowed to rest, that the health of the pilot and the reindeer came first. The Christmas Eve trip was one of the most stressful flights known to man, even more than that of space travel.

As Patrick climbed down, the stablemen immediately went to work, taking the sleigh and looking it over for weak structures and possible stress fractures. The deer were already being looked over by a team of veterinarians, checking vitals and for anything that could be dangerous to their health.

A team of caretakers approached Patrick to check on him, but his mind was stuck on Kris's health. He refused to rest until he was able to speak to him. John Dreiling then approached Patrick to welcome him back. Patrick asked John about Kris's health. John assured Patrick that Kris arrived back at the ranch an hour prior, and that although he was very beaten up, he was in good spirits. John, however, was not able to offer any news about his current condition. Wanting to check up on his master, John took Patrick back to the house, where Kris was being cared for.

As soon as they arrived at the home, he was escorted to Kris's room where they were met by Pinky, who had been watching over him as he recovered. Upon seeing that Patrick was safe, she placed Kris's hand down to his side and then stood to welcome Patrick home. As she walked closer to

Patrick, he could see a look of exhaustion and desperation in her eyes. She hugged Patrick for several moments and then kissed him on the cheek.

Patrick looked Mrs. Claus in the eyes and smiled meekly. "How's he doing ma'am?"

Mrs. Claus wiped the tears from her eyes and paused. Then, with hope in her voice, she answered him. "The doctor said that he took quite a beating, but with plenty of rest, he should be back to normal. He's excited to talk to you and to find out how the rest of the trip went. You saved Christmas, Mr. Wolf. We are all very proud of you, and we recognize the great sacrifices you have made this evening. We will be indebted to you forever."

Mrs. Claus held out her hand, motioning Patrick to sit next to her husband, and then she and John Dreiling left the room.

Patrick removed his stocking hat and placed it against his heart. He then silently walked over to the bed, where Kris was resting. Kris was pale and covered in bandages, protecting his wounds as well as the frostbite he took on, along the way. He looked very weak. As Patrick stood over him, Kris managed to open his eyes, just enough to look over to his new friend and see how he was doing.

Kris smiled weakly, while joy and tears began to well up in his eyes. "You look like crap."

Kris patted the bed and motioned Patrick to sit. Patrick felt so worried for his friend. He smiled at him and then sat down slowly. He sat in the chair and reached over and took his brother by the hand.

Kris was so proud of Patrick. His instinct was correct. Patrick was, indeed, a true Santa. He was so honored that he had the opportunity to meet Patrick Wolf. "Thank you, Patrick. You didn't do too badly for a farm boy. You should be very proud of yourself. Mrs. Claus was right, from this day forward, you will forever be known as the hero who saved Christmas."

Struggling to breathe, Kris paused until he regained his composure. "Did you see her?"

Patrick nodded quietly and sighed.

Kris looked Patrick in the eyes. "I'm so sorry I failed you. I wanted nothing more than for you to go home. I don't really know where to begin thanking you for what you've done."

Kris coughed harshly as he grabbed Patrick's arm tightly. "If there is anything I can ever do to show my appreciation. You gave your life up for us. You are indeed our Christmas present this year."

The tears in Kris's eye flowed over and covered his entire face. "I'm sorry."

Patrick loved his friend like he did his very own brother. He was not disappointed in his friend, nor was he sorry for his decision to save Christmas. "You know what? I know my wife more than anyone, and I know she loves me."

Patrick too, began to cry as he tried to console his loved one. "Someday, when my life is over, and I meet Katie in heaven, she's going to say how proud of me she was for not giving up on a friend. My wife loves me, and I know she'll understand."

Kris suddenly began to cough uncontrollably. The coughing was so rough, that Patrick noticed blood trickling from the corner of his mouth. Standing to his feet, Patrick yelled for the medical staff to help Kris with his cough. As the staff entered the room and ran to Kris's bedside, Patrick pushed his chair to the side and stepped back, just in time to grab Mrs. Claus as she rushed into the room to care for her husband. Kris drifted into unconscious as Mrs. Claus fell onto the bed, next to his side. She pleaded with the staff to take care of him. Repeatedly she yelled to the medics, trying to convince them that Kris was okay, and as she tried to speak life to her husband, fear began to overwhelm her.

Patrick stood silently as the chaos unfolded before him. With the staff working frantically, and Mrs. Claus begging God for his life, Patrick just remained still, allowing the tears to fall from his eyes. Thoughts of his time with Kris passed as he listened to the medical personnel trying to recover their Santa.

Just leaving the house to stay out of the way, Mr. John Dreiling turned to look up towards the window. He began to see shadows bouncing back and forth from behind the curtains. He knew in his heart that such activity in the makeshift emergency room surely meant that his closest friend's health was beginning to fail. He could do nothing but fall to his seat and bow his head in prayer.

For the rest of the world, the sun was beginning to rise. While Patrick stood in shock, children all over the world were waking for Christmas morning.

The doctor and medics worked with Kris to help recover him. And as the world's Santa lay in his bed fighting for his life, millions of youngsters were climbing out of their warm beds, immediately running to the rooms where their packages awaited them.

The rest of the world knew nothing of the disaster that was taking place at the North Pole.

And finally, as Patrick overlooked his Santa and prayed for his life, back at home, Katie was receiving the news about her husband's death

Through an extreme sacrifice, Kris and Patrick's journey had been completed, and Christmas was saved. Even though heartache was rapidly spreading throughout the North Pole ranch, the spirit of Christmas was being celebrated around the world. Christmas had been delivered successfully.

CHAPTER FIFTEEN

Everyone from the North Pole was gathered at the park in front of the toyshop. It had only been a couple weeks prior, when the park was equally full for the Christmas Eve departure. The businesses throughout the North Pole were closed so that everyone could take part in the celebration of Kris's life, as well as giving their support to Mrs. Claus.

The crowd soon came to a hush, as a faint drum cadence began to echo throughout the city. Sitting in a carriage, half way down the path from the toyshop, Patrick, Mrs. Claus, and John Dreiling watched as two drum lines made their way from the workshop, out into the forecourt. Once the drum corps had come together as a unit, they continued in tempo as their drum major marched forward, until he came to the spot in front of Mrs. Claus. He soon took his place and then he stopped to blow his whistle, bringing the entire drum line to a stop.

The entire city was so quiet you could hear a pin drop. Kris had been loved by everyone. There wasn't a heart he had not touched.

As the drum corps remained at attention, the drum major turned to Mrs. Claus and with a slow salute, a loan bagpiper, marched from where the drum line was formed and slowly walked forward until reaching the drum major, out at the front of the procession. The piper continued to play until reaching the end of the hymn.

Once the song had ended, the piper turned and walked ahead of the drum corps, twenty paces down the drive, putting him out front of everyone.

After the two men found their place, a woman walked up to a podium across the path, where a microphone awaited her. The woman took a deep nervous breath and then smiled nervously, acknowledging Mrs. Claus. She than began to sing a melody more beautiful than anything Patrick had ever heard before. As she sang, it was as if the northern lights began to flash through the sky upon the command of her voice. As the singer's voice climbed through the octaves, the lights became brighter, and as the singer began to sing in a lower range, the lights grew darker.

The loan piper joined her in concert and the two formed a majestic melody. In complete harmony, the streets echoed with beauty that grabbed the hearts of everyone present.

The drum major began to blow his whistle and raised his rod. The second his staff touch the sky, the large doors to the toyshop began to open, where Santa's sleigh appeared from inside, just like it had on Christmas Eve. Everyone in the city stood to their feet as Santa appeared, preparing his final mission.

The drum major then commanded his corps to begin beating their drums in rhythm to the music, and then on his count, they began to march forward, officially beginning the ceremonies. As the drum line move forward, the sounds of bagpipes started ringing throughout the park from inside the toyshop. As the woman continued to sing in praise, the piper, the drum major, and his drum line, all marched in tune. Behind them, a thousand bag pipers slowly emerged from the toyshop, directly behind the drum line. As they marched, the music grew louder and louder, echoing pure bliss throughout the sky.

Once the entire parade was in order and the last pipers had left the toyshop, Santa's reindeer took action and proudly marched forward, following the corps with their leader, one final time.

As the entire procession passed by Mrs. Claus and her companions, Pinky found it almost too difficult to keep her royal Claus-like composure. Mrs. Claus's eyes welled up as she watched her husband draw closer. Patrick reached around her and embraced her as she saw the sight of her husband's casket. Draped in a blanket of red silk, and with Santa's hat resting on top, Pinky broke down, homesick for her husband. Patrick handed Mrs. Claus a handkerchief for her eyes. He then looked to Santa and gently waved goodbye to him. Once the sleigh had passed, Patrick and Mrs. Claus held on to the carriage where they had been sitting. Mr. John Dreiling commanded the horses that were pulling the carriage, to get in place, lining up to follow behind Santa.

Seeing the looks of remorse in everyone as they rode behind Santa's sleigh, Patrick could not help but to wonder about his own funeral service back at home. He was sorry that he had left Katie but knew she would have been proud of him for putting Christmas first. Patrick knew that he was missed by his family, and he was going to miss them very much. He was also going to miss everyone back at home.

The entire cortege was on their way down the park drive towards the heart of the city, where the Tree of Life stood. Thousands upon thousands of the elves had lined the streets to pay homage to the Clauses. Today, everyone at the North Pole was in morning for their Santa but in celebration for the life he led.

Arriving at the Tree of Life, the entire musical parade made their way to their appointed locations, surrounding the square. Santa's reindeer pulled the sleigh to the center of the square where the sleigh of Patrick and Mrs. Claus pulled up behind. Patrick and John Dreiling escorted Mrs. Claus to their seats. The entire crowd stood for Pinky in Respect for her. Then, once Pinky sat in her seat, the rest of the elves, respectfully followed her lead. The memorial service for Santa was ready to begin.

As the pastor spoke of Santa and his life, a welcomed laughter began to fill the air. Patrick had never witnessed such a wonderful service. Stories of his life were shared. Not stories of grief but only about how he had changed the lives of everyone, for the better of the world.

One final prayer was given for Santa, and then Mrs. Claus was allowed to approach the casket to say farewell. Once again, the streets were hushed as Mrs. Claus walked up to Santa and laid her hands on the casket. Mrs. Claus wept as she proclaimed her undying love for her husband. She also assured him that she would see him again in heaven, and that she hoped he would wait for her. With both of her hands, she leaned against the casket, and kissed it gently. She then closed her eyes and said one final goodbye. Patrick stood to his feet as Pinky was then escorted back to her seat, where he remained with her, just like family.

A small group of Santa's men, including John Dreiling, approached the sleigh and surrounded Santa. Once again, the woman began to sing as the men removed Santa's hat and removed the draping silk from the casket. As the men slowly folded the fabric, John Dreiling proudly stood still with Santa's hat in his arms. The men took the silk and made a teddy bear out of the fabric, using much of Santa's hardware as accessories to use on the bear. Once finished, the men carried the bear to John, where he slowly placed Santa's hat on the bear. He then broke ceremony for only a moment and kissed the bear on the cheek. Taking the teddy bear into his grasp, Mr. Dreiling walked back towards Mrs. Claus and stood before her.

John looked her in the eyes and smiled gently. "Mr. Christkind and I have spent many years together. He was my finest friend. It is with great sorrow that we are here, but then again, it is my greatest honor that I present to you this token of our love for you both. Hold him dearly. His ashes have been placed in this bear's heart."

Mr. John Dreiling reached out his arms, holding the bear out in front of him. As Pinky reached out to receive the bear, the elves in the drum corps saluted Mrs. Claus. Mrs. Claus loved teddy bears more than any other form of toy. Her heart overflowed with humility, knowing that everyone remembered. She reached out and took the bear and then, just like a young child, brought the bear in close to her chest and held him tightly as she began to cry uncontrollably.

John then returned to his seat as the pastor gave one final prayer. The drum line began their cadence in rhythm, joined by the army of bagpipes, who all performed gloriously for their fallen leader. The Tree of life began to light up brightly as the lights twinkled. The reindeer became anxious as they scraped their hooves on the ground and rocked their heads. They then began to move forward; slowly making one final pass around the square so that everyone could wave to Santa, one last time. On their final turn, the tree of light began to shine rays of light into the dark sky. The reindeer then rushed forward and launched into the air, circling the Tree of Life, gaining in speed and widening their radius until they finally launched into the sky leaving a trail of northern lights behind them, and disappearing into the polar night sky. The entire city erupted with celebration as flakes of light began to fall over the city, left behind from the sleigh. Sorrow became joy as everyone was left in awe, and Santa was taken to heaven.

As the last flakes of light fell, and the music began to come to an end, Mrs. Claus grabbed Patrick by the hand. She then pulled him out in front of the crowd so that she could thank him appropriately for the sacrifices he had made this Christmas.

Mrs. Claus looked at Patrick and stood before him. Although, she was full of sorrow, she was very pleased for what Patrick had done for her and Santa, and she wanted to show her kindness to him with the elves as her witnesses.

Mrs. Claus smiled at her friends and commenced in appreciation. "Patrick Wolf, this year, you showed us the true spirit of Christmas. You have saved Christmas, and we will be eternally grateful for your display of heroism. Please allow me to present to you the highest award the North Pole has to offer."

Mrs. Claus stepped aside and held out her hand towards the Tree of life, where three womanly figures appeared. Dressed in white the caped figures ceremonially raised their arms, each holding precious gifts. They then began to walk forward, until reaching the spot where she and Patrick stood.

Patrick smiled. He was so proud of what he had accomplished, but was not sure that such an award was deserved.

As the women approached, the elves began to quietly murmur with suspense.

Mrs. Claus turned and stood in front of the women. She then reached out to the first woman and gently removed a garment from her hands, and turned towards Patrick.

Pinky looked Patrick in the eyes and smiled brightly. "Now, if you would please remove your coat for me."

Patrick did as Mrs. Claus wished. As he removed his coat, John Dreiling stepped in to assist Patrick, taking it from him and holding it.

Mrs. Claus spoke with great pride for her friend and brother. "Patrick, on behalf of Santa and me, please except this coat that we have prepared for you."

Mrs. Claus raised the coat and presented it to Patrick. It was his coat from home that he wore when he played Santa. The leather and fur had been completely restored. The colors were bright and not one blemish could be seen. It was as if his coat was brand new again. Patrick was honored. He turned around so that Mrs. Clause could place the coat on him. Patting him on the shoulder, he then returned back around, facing Mrs. Claus once again.

Mrs. Clause then reached over to the second woman and took the garment from her hands. It was Patrick's Santa hat. It too had been restored to new. Patrick recognized it right away and shed a tear as the wonderful Christmas memories came back to him. No longer were they full of sorrow as they had become over the years, instead, they were remembrances of joy and hope, knowing that he had helped to keep the Christmas Spirit alive in the town of Ellinwood. Finally, Patrick understood that Christmas was not lost but very much alive.

Mrs. Claus held the furry hat up high and placed it on Patrick's head. The villagers became excited as Patrick stood before them in the cherished Santa uniform. Trying to contain themselves, they remained silent as the ceremony proceeded.

Mrs. Claus stood back and looked at Patrick. She could see the same spirit in him that she saw in her husband. She was full of honor. "You look very sharp my friend. You remind me of Santa, whom I will always love from the bottom of my heart. I have just one more gift for you."

Mrs. Claus stepped to the side as the third woman stepped up with a medal in her hand, resting on top of a tiny box. She approached Patrick and raised it to his chest.

The murmuring stopped, and the entire city became quiet with anticipation.

Mrs. Claus began to cry with joy as the woman pinned Patrick's coat with the highest award the North Pole could offer, the medal of Santa.

Once the medal was placed on to Patrick's coat the woman held up the tiny box that was designed to accompany the medal. Patrick looked down as she opened the box for him. As soon as he saw what lay inside, Patrick's eyes clamped shut with elation. Inside the box was the ring that Patrick left for Katie on Christmas Eve. He looked up at the woman as she unveiled herself and looked into Patrick's eyes.

Patrick began to cry as he recognized Katie, standing before him. Without hesitation, Patrick grabbed his wife and embraced her, engaging her with a passionate kiss.

With a smile, Pinky spoke joyfully on behalf of herself and all the people throughout the land. "Ladies and gentlemen, I present to you, your new Mr. and Mrs. Santa Claus!"

As soon as Pinky made the announcement, fireworks illuminated the sky, and a loud roar filled the streets of the North Pole with cheers of celebration.

Patrick looked into the eyes of his cherished bride and presented her with the exact same smile that he shared with her from the very beginning of their marriage.

Katie glowed with love for her newly found husband and Santa. "I love you!"

Before Patrick could even ask, out of the joyous crowd, the couple was met by their children and grandchildren. Patrick hugged each and every one of them and laughed with joy. Patrick was complete again.

Christmas had been saved.

THE END

———— · *W* · ————

"Merry Christmas!"

\